BACKCHECK HEART

KAT SUMMERS

This book is a work of fiction from the author's imagination. Though inspired by the world around us, all of the characters, places, and events are fictional and not based on any one source. Any resemblance is entirely coincidental.

Backcheck Heart

Edited by Emma Jane of EJL Editing

Proofed by Caroline Palmier

Cover Illustration by Booked Forever

NOTE FROM THE AUTHOR/DICKTIONARY

Backcheck Heart is a feel-good hockey novella but does deal with issues of low self-esteem, a manipulative ex, and hockey fights.

Though a short read, I hope this story resonates, delights, or entertains you. It is an off-shoot of the Nashville Songbirds series. While there are currently no other LA Crush books planned, that could change if there is interest!

Looking for the spice?

Find it in chapters 9, 10, and 14!

ONE

Morgan

"FIRST ROUND, BITCHESSSSS," I yell as I spray the screaming crowd with champagne. They don't understand why we're excited, but drunk people will cheer for anything.

"He got the call?" my coworker, Tammy, asks once my bottle is depleted.

"Seattle, baby! My little *Bobert* is going to the big leagues!" I exclaim. Minutes ago, my younger brother, Rob, was picked by the Seattle Eagles in the first round of the MLB draft. As much as I wish I could hug him right now, he is at the official draft event with his girlfriend, Carina. I will have to settle for celebrating with the rowdy patrons of Clamatis—the downtown LA nightclub where I work as a bottle girl when I'm in between assignments as a flight attendant.

My bubbly personality makes me an excellent fit for both roles. Working for the airline, I visit places I'd never be able to otherwise. My server-slash-influencer side gig gets me in the doors at some of the most exclusive parties in LA, surrounded by the rich and famous. My

1

ability to date Leonardo Dicaprio may be dwindling with my twenty-fifth birthday on the horizon, but I am having a blast.

If my career is right where I want it, my love life is a million miles away. I wouldn't know a nice guy if he slapped me on the ass. The ones who are slapping me on the ass leave a lot to be desired, including my current situationship, Chet. He's… fine. Most of the time. He has a habit of acting as if he's better than me because he went to college. God forbid I point out that I make more money doing my 'pretty girl' jobs than he does in finance. He's been weird about putting a label on our relationship, but it doesn't stop him from taking advantage of boyfriend privileges.

Like most nights at work at Clamatis, Chet and his buddies take up a corner booth, hoping I'll sneak them unused bottles. For men who claim to be rolling in dough, they sure love free shit. More than that, they love the way women perceive them while they get their free shit. Chet and I have had more than one blowout over him getting too friendly with the girls his friends invite. Thankfully, the other club I work at is too pricey for them to hang out at.

Pushing Chet's antics out of my mind, I think about how proud I am of my brother. He has been working for this moment almost his entire life, and he finally made it happen. I am excited for him to live his dream but sad that I won't have my buddy around when he moves to Texas to join the minor league team. At least I have two more years with his girlfriend to keep me company.

Putting down the cheap champagne I used to shower the crowd, I grab a nice bottle of Vevue to take over to a table of new arrivals. When I do, I am greeted by the sight of eight sexy walls of muscle. I don't know who these guys are, but they are definitely athletes. I'd guess football. Schooling my expression into a bright smile, I approach their booth.

"Hey, boys. Welcome to Clamatis. My name is Morgan. I'll be helping you out tonight. Please let me or one of the other servers know if you need anything. And enjoy this complimentary bottle from the manager."

"Hello, beautiful," one of the guys replies. He is huge. His dark hair is the right amount of unruly, and scruff covers his jaw. "I'm

Connor. We're here to celebrate this guy's upcoming wedding, so please keep the drinks flowing."

He plants his hand on the shoulder of a slightly smaller—if you can call a six-foot Adonis small— blond who smiles back at me.

"Congratulations, Mr. Groom," I reply. "Your fiancée is a lucky lady."

He flushes at the compliment. My heart clenches at how adorable the sight of a guy that manly getting embarrassed is. As I scan the rest of the group, my eyes stop on the man sitting at the far end of the booth. And when I say man, I mean *man*. This guy exudes masculinity and BDE in a way I can't explain. His vibe says, "Don't fuck with me," but my messed up brain is begging me to.

Dark blue eyes stare back at me under thick brows. His hair is cropped short to match his beard, and he has an air of intensity surrounding him. He's more serious than the rest of the group, evident by his slight scowl.

"Cheer up, big guy," I direct at him. "Your friend is getting married."

He blinks at me as if he is shocked I spoke to him. His gaze holds me hostage. I don't look away until someone else in the group speaks.

"Don't mind Wreck-It Ralph. That's just his face. He's what we in the biz call 'a grump.'"

"Wreck-It Ralph? Like the cartoon?" I ask.

"Yep," Connor replies, popping his 'p.' "Nokavik here can bust through any defenseman in the NHL."

"Ah, hockey players. I should have known. I would have put my money on football."

The group lets out a collective gasp. "That is an insult where we come from, sweetheart," one of the other guys states.

"My sincerest apologies. Please accept this free bottle you were already going to get as restitution," I tease. The man they call Ralph's lips tip up the tiniest amount at my words, and I vow to get a full smile out of him before the night is over.

"I'll be back to check on you boys later. In the meantime, don't have too much fun without me."

"We wouldn't dream of it," someone responds.

Throughout the night, I float between groups, lingering longest at the table of hockey players. I've charmed most of them but haven't cracked Ralphie—the name I've dubbed him in my head. I added the '-ie' for my own enjoyment.

On a quick trip to the bathroom, I Googled the roster of the local NHL team, the LA Crush. Ralphie's actual name is Radek Nokavik. As a believer in name manifestation, I can't accept that the grump of the bunch has a name that means 'happy.' Ralph is much more fitting with its meaning of 'wolf counsel.' The way his eyes track my movements screams calculated predator.

"You all doing okay?" I ask as I approach the group again later in the night.

"We are doing spectacular, gorgeous," Troy, the flirtiest of them, answers. Ralphie's frown deepens at the interaction.

"Happy to hear it," I reply. Glancing around to ensure all my other booths are taken care of, I waltz into their section and plant myself next to the grouch I am determined to soften.

"What can we do to turn that frown upside down, Ralphie?"

His brow quirks, but he doesn't say anything about the nickname. "I'm doing fine," he says in a deep, accented voice. This is the first time I've heard him speak. From my online stalking, I knew he was from the Czech Republic, but I am delighted to hear how thick his accent still is.

"You say that, but your face disagrees," I counter. "You want water? Have a song request for the DJ? Oh! How about body shots?"

I see the other guys perk up, but Ralphie rushes out an immediate, "No. Clothes stay on."

"Geez, way to save a girl's ego," I murmur. "We have designated servers for that, but I will keep my clothes on around you, Nokavik."

His eyes darken before he shakes off whatever emotion was clouding them. "You know who I am?"

"I may have done some light Googling," I admit with a hair flip. "I wanted to figure out if you were always this frowny or if it was me."

I cringe as my tone gives a hint of vulnerability. I don't need to broadcast my people pleasing tendencies to this stranger. Stuffing my insecurities back into a box, I plaster on a smile. I'm interrupted as I rack my brain for something to change the subject.

"You don't make me frown, *Zlatíčko*. This is my happy face, see." His face remains impassive, and I'm confused until it dawns on me that he is teasing.

"Are you-did you make a joke?" I question slowly.

"Maybe." He shrugs, but his mouth tugs into an almost grin. I beam in victory.

"Much better," he says, taking in my delight. "There's your real smile."

"My real smile?"

"You've been doling out smiles all night, but they aren't all the same. From what I can see, you have your amused smile, customer service smile, and genuine smile that shines so bright it is as if you can't keep it off your face."

Damn, heavy stuff from the big guy. I didn't realize he was paying such close attention to me. Most people don't see past my bubbly, blonde facade, but he has. The thought that I was that transparent makes me squirm.

Patting him on the knee, I wink and say, "I should go see if there is anyone else's night I can brighten."

I scramble out of the booth. Despite the win, the interaction exposed something in me that I try to lock down tight. Typically, my party girl persona keeps people at bay, but not Ralphie. He brought out more from me than I intended.

I make a point to put space between us for the rest of the evening. Thankfully, the night gets busy after that. That doesn't stop me from sneaking glances at a certain booth when I have a moment, though. Several times, I catch him shamelessly watching me back.

The next time it happens, our staring contest is broken by my manager, Greg.

"Morgan, your boyfriend and his friends are getting out of hand. They need to chill out, or I'm booting them."

Fuck. With my attention on the hockey hunks, I forgot to keep an eye on Chet and his friends. "I am so sorry. I will go take care of it."

He nods and walks away to handle the other million and one issues he is dealing with tonight. I hate that I was one of them.

"Chet!" I shout when I get over to his section.

Glassy-eyed, he turns to face me. "Babe, there you are! We need another bottle."

"You guys are done for the night," I state. "You need to keep it down. Otherwise, Greg is going to kick you out."

"What? We aren't doing anything! That prick needs to lighten up."

"That *prick* is my boss. If you're going to get me in trouble, I won't get you in anymore."

"Pssh, this isn't your main job. You don't need this place. You're too hot to be a server, anyway. You should be partying with me."

"Chet, I enjoy this job. You're embarrassing me," I grit.

"*I'm* embarrassing *you*?" he slurs. "I'm the one who had to watch my girl hang all over some fucking douchebags all night. You think I want my friends to see you slutting yourself out to sell drinks?"

He moved in front of me at some point during his tirade. In my heels, we're practically the same height, but his words make me feel two feet tall. What partner talks to you that way?

I back away to give myself more room, but I hit a firm chest.

"Everything okay?" someone rumbles from behind me. I know immediately who it is from the accent. When I look over my shoulder, Ralphie is studying Chet with suspicion.

"Everything is fine," Chet sneers. "She may have been flirting with you for tips all night, but she's taken. Back off."

Chet's claim makes me bristle. We see each other once or twice a week after he gets off work and then at Clamatis on Saturday nights. He is more of a glorified booty call than anything. I've pushed for more, but he wants to 'focus on his career' right now. The fact that he is getting territorial is laughable.

Ralphie looks at me for confirmation, which I don't give. I don't deny it, either. Haven't I been mooning over book boyfriends who get growly for years? Maybe this will be a turning point. It feels wrong that it's Chet, but I will take what I can get.

"Thank you for checking on me," I say to Ralphie, hoping it tells him I'm okay.

With another perusal of the man who has now slung his arm over my shoulder, the broody hockey player gives a curt nod and heads off toward the bathrooms. I exhale a sharp breath and shrug off Chet.

"Are you calming down or going home?" I question.

"We'll be chill. You get off soon, right? I can't wait to get you home." I fight a shiver as he nuzzles into my neck.

I tell him I should be done in an hour, disappointed he can't tell it's my difficult customer smile. Hopefully, he and his friends will get bored without more free drinks and leave before my shift ends. My gaze travels back to the hockey booth, but they're surrounded by beautiful women on the dance floor.

My chest pangs in disappointment that I may not lock with those watchful navy eyes again. But I know they will haunt my dreams.

TWO

Ralphie

I CANNOT BELIEVE a woman that beautiful is with that sloppy idiot. Not only is she gorgeous, but her charm and sunny demeanor had even my grumpy ass *almost* smiling. At least, I was until I saw that red-faced fuck boy spewing spittle at her. Her obvious embarrassment was enough to have me out of my seat and across the VIP area before I knew what I was doing.

I couldn't believe it when she waved me off. She didn't confirm they were a couple, but she didn't deny it either. I may not know her, but she can do much better than that chump.

"Better luck next time, bud," Connor says with a slap on my shoulder when I settle next to him on the outskirts of the dance floor. I don't reply, but he doesn't expect me to.

Everyone was surprised that I came out tonight. I was shocked when I heard the "yes" come out of my mouth, but I figured it was better than sitting at home. In the offseason, aside from my daily work-outs, I don't have much going on. Fitz's wedding is the only thing on my calendar until training camp in August.

Plus, my agent, Andre, says I need to bond more with the team so management knows I want to stick around. There have been trade rumors, and he wants me to seem 'settled' in the community, whatever that means. He even suggested a fake PR relationship, but I shot that down quickly.

The guys buzz around me, talking and drinking as I nurse my beer. My gaze follows Morgan as she floats from group to group.

I haven't been this enraptured by a woman, maybe ever. The braid in her honey hair circles her head like a crown, which is apt, seeing as she resembles a goddess to me. Each table lights up when she stops and chats with them. Something about her disarms everyone around her. A couple of women give her side eye when the men they're with linger on her too long, but I can't blame them. I don't know how every eye in the room doesn't stay glued to her like mine.

Sometime later, her supposed boyfriend leaves with his buddies, slapping her ass on the way out and whispering something that makes her pinch her lips. I'm glad to see she isn't enamored by his pompous persona. He is clearly the type to put on a show for his friends. I watch her body lose tension as his friends help him out the door.

She should be with someone who relieves her stress, not causes it. I don't realize I'm clutching my drink as I stare at her until Fitz speaks beside me. "Whoa, big guy. You'll break the bottle if you grip it any tighter."

I immediately loosen my hold.

"She's cute," he notes, laughing when I shoot a glare his way. "Not for me. Tabby is more than enough for me to handle. Trust me. You should ask her out, though. I've never seen you pay a woman half as much attention as you have her."

"She has a boyfriend," I grumble.

"The overgrown frat boy?"

I nod in response.

"Based on everything I saw tonight, I don't think it would take much for her to trade up, my friend. Shoot your shot. The worst she can say is no. At the very least, it might get her thinking there are better options out there than that douche canoe. Besides, no one scores against a goalie better than you."

"Maybe," I hedge. I would typically never hit on a taken woman, but she didn't confirm his claim on her earlier. He could have been overinflating their relationship. Fitz knows I would never help someone cheat, but that doesn't mean I can't find out for sure if she's in a relationship or not.

"Come on." He nudges my arm. "I'll cover for you with the guys while you ask for her number."

I shake my head at my friend and teammate. "We're here to honor you tonight, not pick up chicks."

"The best way you can celebrate me is to find someone to settle down with. None of these other guys are anywhere near ready to slow down the party lifestyle, but you've never been one to indulge much in that. Join me on the dark, committed as fuck side."

"Tabby is a lucky girl," I tell him.

"Nah, I'm the lucky one. I'm just glad I'm locking her down before all these hits to the head catch up to me, and I skate my way across the entire US, Forest Gump-style.

"What?"

"Nothing," he claps. "Diversion time."

Standing up, he walks to the other end of the booth and shouts, "The groom-to-be needs a shot. Who's buying?"

As the rest of the group clamors to ply Fitz with liquor, I sneak out, catching his wink on my way. With a salute back at him, I head in the direction Morgan went a few minutes ago.

Opening the door I watched her pass through, my eyes take a minute to adjust to the change from dark club lighting. I find myself in a hallway with six doors. I study each as if they will have a tell as to which one she went into. Before I hazard a guess, one opens to my right, and the girl working with Morgan steps out. She's changed out of her slinky dress and into leggings and a casual tee.

"Hey there, handsome," she croons. "Can I help you with something? You aren't supposed to be back here."

Gripping the back of my neck, I struggle for an answer that won't come off stalkerish.

"Looking for Morgan?" she asks, having mercy on me. I nod. "She left already."

I deflate at the news. Damn. I was hoping I'd get to talk to her again.

"Okay," I reply, turning to leave.

"She'll be working her other job for the next four days but should be back here next weekend if everything goes as planned," the Raven-haired server calls after me.

"What?"

"This is her side gig. She works here around her main job's schedule. She is here on Saturdays when she can be. If she's free during the week, she usually works at Two-One-Oh. It's in Hollywood."

"Why are you telling me all this?" I question. Does her friend normally give strangers her daily schedule? That's concerning and not at all safe.

She laughs. "I saw the way you watched her all night. Your eyes didn't stray to another woman once. That's already more than I can say for Chet. Morgan is sweet but doesn't realize she could do way better than that loser. I figure you can't be any worse."

"Thanks?" The bar to being better than Chet–a befitting name based on his douchey appearance–is low, but I'll take it.

"Just remember to invite me to the wedding," she singsongs. "You should get out of here before Greg catches you. He's testier than usual tonight."

"Got it. Thanks again," I say as I hustle out the door.

From behind me, I hear a whispered, "Bye, Ralphie." The smile that had been threatening to break free all night finally does when I realize she talked to her friend about me. I may have a chance after all.

I SPEND the next two weeks thinking about Morgan. I returned to Clamatis the next Saturday night but didn't see either of the women who worked the previous week. They either weren't scheduled or were working the "V-VIP" party I heard murmurs about from other clubgoers. Uninterested in anyone but the gorgeous blonde taking up residence in my brain, I didn't stick around to see who would be considered very, very important.

I won't be able to hit up Clamatis this weekend because it is Fitz's wedding. Today, I am flying to Turks and Caicos to attend their nuptials. I was offered a plus one, but I declined. The only woman I've given a second glance to in the last several years has vanished into thin air. At least, that's what I thought until I am met with a pair of familiar blue eyes as I settle into my first class seat. They widen in shock as they take me in.

Our gazes remain locked until the sound of someone slamming the overhead bin ends our stare down.

"Hi," she rushes out, as stunned as I am. She glances at the glass in her hand as if attempting to remember why she is here. "Can I get you anything? Champagne?"

"Are body shots on the menu this time?"

Morgan chokes on a laugh. "Not on this airline. That's more of a Spirit thing."

I can't stop my lips from tipping at her quick reply. "I'll have to remember that next time I book."

I want to say more, but someone further back motions that they want champagne. With an apologetic smile, she shuffles off to serve them. It's for the best that she went away before I blurted out something embarrassing about going back to the club or how close I was to asking my agent to track her number down. If he wouldn't have made a big deal about it, I may have asked.

She steals peeks at me throughout her pre-flight service and safety demonstration. I know because my gaze hasn't left her since I first realized she was the attendant on this flight. I normally hate flying. I usually feel trapped in the tiny seats. But being in an enclosed space with Morgan is worth the cramped quarters.

Because I'm watching her like a creep, I don't miss her interaction with a mother flying solo with two children on the other side of the plane. With a baby in her lap, the woman is struggling to calm down the toddler, who is uncomfortable with the change in altitude. Instead of giving the woman an annoyed glare like some passengers, Morgan goes into her cubby and pulls out a green frog. The little boy squeals in delight when she hands it to him. Happily playing with his new toy, he's forgotten his discomfort.

When she is back in front of me to take my lunch order, I blurt out the first question that pops into my mind, desperate to keep her with me for as long as possible. "Do you always carry toys with you?"

"What?" she asks, oblivious that I saw the earlier exchange.

"You gave that little boy a toy when he was crying. Is that something the airline does, or is that a *you* thing?"

She blushes and quickly peers away. And fuck, if it doesn't do something to me. The fact that a woman this beautiful can still blush is adorable.

"It's a 'me thing,' I guess." She shrugs. "Other people do it, too, in some variation, usually with crayons and coloring books. Giving them a distraction can help shift a kid's mood. Flying is stressful for them. It's stressful for adults, too, but at least we understand what is happening. They don't."

"You just hit up a toy store to stay stocked with goodies?"

"Oh, um, I made it actually."

My brows raise. I peek around her to get a better look at the frog. It's hard to tell from this far away, but it appears to be made from yarn.

"You made that?" I ask, the shock evident in my voice.

The pink in her cheeks deepens. "Yeah, it's not all that hard, unlike cardigans."

"How did you learn?"

"My grandmother taught me," she replies brightly. "I spent a lot of time with her when I was young, and she liked to say, 'You can't always count on a man to keep you warm. A young lady should know how to do that herself.' And then she taught me how to crochet.'"

Morgan smiles at the memory despite her watery eyes. I reach out and place my hands over hers, returning the expression. "That's amazing."

"Thank you," she responds genuinely. "Most people think crocheting is a silly hobby in California, but there is much more you can make than blankets and sweaters."

Before I can further engage her, her coworker comes to help deliver lunch orders. Despite the flight's length, we can only get a few minutes here and there to chat. I didn't think to ask for her number until it was too late. I am clearly out of practice. I linger after I deplane, but my driver has already been here twenty minutes and I don't want to keep him waiting. Reluctantly, I make my way through the airport and hope she'll be on my return flight.

THREE

TAMMY TOLD me Ralphie came after me that night at Clamatis, but I never expected to see him again. He's an NHL superstar. I'm the daughter of a plumber who makes half her income pouring liquor straight into people's mouths. We aren't cut from the same cloth. Still, it was flattering that he wanted to talk to me again.

It almost made up for the incoherent drunk texts I got from Mr. Suddenly Wants A Label Now That Someone Else Appears Interested. It's wearing on me more and more that Chet decided we were in a relationship when he doesn't treat me any better than a booty call most of the time. I can count the times I've seen him between 9 a.m. and 9 p.m. on one hand. I don't especially want to be alone, but surely I deserve more than being strung along by the likes of Chet Daniels.

As if I needed a reminder that there are still nice guys out there, the big broody hockey player was on my flight. I was pleasantly surprised that he was more conversational than the last time I saw him. In fact, I almost dropped the flute I was holding when he made his joke about body shots. Something tells me he doesn't joke often.

I was surprised when he asked me about the frog I gave to the crying little boy. Not because he was watching me—I could sense the weight of his stare the entire flight—but because no one besides my family has ever talked about crocheting with me.

After one of my so-called friends laughed in my face at a beach party when I told her I crocheted my cover-up, I stopped mentioning it. Anytime Chet sees my supplies, he says I'm 'too young and hot to be doing old lady shit.' But here is this big hunk of Czech man candy complimenting it and asking to know *more*. I don't know what to do with that.

Despite the almost five-hour flight, we were only able to talk a handful of times. Weekday travelers are extra needy, and that group was no exception. I'm thankful that I am off for a few days after the return flight this morning. I got home too late to work at Two-One-Oh, which I count as a blessing. I could use a break, especially since I'll be at Clamatis tomorrow night.

Taking advantage of Madison's absence, I curl up on my couch to watch *Big Bang Theory*. I love a show that has a bubbly blonde surrounded by unlikely friends. On this show, her brainiac friends see her for more than her appearance—most of the time. They treated each other with respect and kindness despite her not being as book-smart as them, and she even taught them some lessons along the way.

Shifting through my crocheting supplies, I pull out a half-finished bunny to replace the frog I gave away. I end up putting it back in the bag and searching for a new pattern on Pinterest. I could use a challenge. Seeing a beanie with a cute pom pom, I think it may be the ticket. And if I happen to choose the colors of the LA Crush, that is purely a coincidence.

THE CLUB IS WILD TONIGHT. A guest DJ is in town, and he brought his supermodel girlfriend and her posse. I've never seen the VIP section this packed. It was too busy to snag Chet and his friends a table. Based on the buzzing from my smart watch, he is still pissed about it. I can't help that paying customers pre-booked the booths, not that he'll care.

As usual, I flit from table to table to make sure everyone is taken care of. I chat with a few models, who are nicer than I expected, and some MLB players who came out after their game. I tell them about Rob and to be on the lookout for him in a few years. They tried to get my number in the name of 'advising' him, but even I'm not dumb enough to fall for that trick.

Back in the locker room, I sigh as I take off my heels and change into comfy clothes. I space out the entire drive home, thinking about how excited I am to see my bed. My evening plans are dashed when I spot an obnoxiously expensive car idling in the parking space outside my apartment. Of course, Chet parked in *my* spot, forcing me to park in the creepy corner. Eyeing my front door, I wonder if there is a way to sneak past him, but the door of his Audi opens as I approach.

Blowing out a raspberry, I face the music of whatever his issue is today. At least I'm not alone as I make the longer-than-it-should-have-been walk to my apartment. Clocking his pinched expression, I wonder if I ever found him hot or just craved the attention. He's in decent shape and dresses well—if finance bro is your type—but the longer we've been 'together,' the less attractive I've found him.

"What are you doing here?" I ask exasperated.

"I wanted to make sure my girlfriend made it home."

Oh, that's sweet.

"And didn't end up in bed between whatever overgrown jocks you were slobbering over all night."

There it is. I should have seen the insult coming, but it still stings. You can say a lot of bad things about me, but that I would be unfaithful isn't one of them. And last time I checked, despite calling himself my boyfriend, we never had the exclusivity talk. I'd point that out, but it would only prolong this confrontation, and I desperately want to shower and sleep. Exhausted from a long slip, my filter fails and uncharacteristic sass slips through.

"Did you drive all the way across town to be a dick?" I snap. "If you think that lowly of me, why are you wasting your time?"

"I'm wasting my time because I see your potential." Ouch. I know I said it first, but I don't want to be considered a 'waste of time.'

"Potential for what?"

"To be the ideal wife. You're hot, a great cook, and stacked. If you could tone down your personality and stop waving your tits in the face of every rich dude you see, you could be something."

"Tone down?" I repeat. I should probably be more upset about the other things he said, but that part stuck out in my mind. "What do you mean by that?"

"You're too much, ninety-nine percent of the time. Too loud, too bright, too perky. You would be the perfect mate if you learn to be more demure, less everything else."

'The perfect mate?' The audacity of this man. I can't believe *he* has the gall to want perfection from *me*. The man is balding, drunk half the time, and living way above his means. He has no room to talk.

"Again, why are you with me if that's what you think of me?"

"I'm no quitter. I've already put so much work into training you. I'd be a shame to throw in the towel now."

"Training me?" I shriek, not caring if I wake up my neighbors.

"Calm down! See, this is what I mean about being too loud. And yes, training you. You think you cut out bread and stopped wearing red lipstick on your own? That was all me, honey."

The realization hits me like a punch to the gut. He has been 'training' me, or at the very least molding me. And I let him without realizing it. I cut back on gluten when he suggested it would help with my acne flare-ups. I stopped wearing red lipstick when he mentioned it was 'too cliche.' That fucker has been manipulating me for months.

Mistaking the shock for something else—gratitude, maybe?—he strokes the side of my face as I recall other ways he's been controlling my life like when he convinced me a CRV was a better investment than the Beetle I wanted. He also talked me out of applying for an international promotion because he 'wouldn't get to see me as much.'

Rage courses through me as I push him away. "Consider your pet project over, Chet. I deserve someone who likes me for me. Not who wants to engineer me into some idealized non-person."

"Don't be ridiculous, babe. You're not breaking up with me. I'm the best you'll ever get."

"I'll take my chances," I mutter, entirely over his shit. Walking past him, I march toward my door. Before I make it out of reach, he grabs my wrist and yanks me back, hard.

"I'm not done talking to you, Morgan," he spits in my face. "I sure as fuck am not about to be dumped by some cosmetology school dropout."

"I—"

"I'm still not done," he sneers, tightening his grip. "That mouth is only good for one thing, and it isn't talking. If you think I'm going to let your little temper tantrum ruin my image by having *you* break up with *me*, you have another thing coming. You're lucky a guy of my status gave you the time of day."

I whimper at his painful hold, but he doesn't loosen it. The ferocity in his expression isn't something I've experienced before—from him or any man. My dad may have yelled at me as a kid, but even when I took his car out for a joyride at fifteen, he didn't spew this much vitriol. The energy pulsing off Chet is scaring me. I need to get away from him. Before I have to devise a plan, the door beside mine opens.

"Hey assholes, people are trying to sleep," my neighbor, Darren, yells. Darren moved to LA to be an actor but grew up in Nebraska. He's what he likes to call 'farm strong.' He stays fit thanks to his day job in construction. Chet's lean but lacks the muscle Darren has on full display in all his cut-off-sweatpants-glory.

I don't stick around when Chet drops my arm to see how the conversation ends. I hightail it inside and lock the door behind me. Crawling into bed without changing, I cradle my arm and cry myself to sleep. The tears aren't over losing Chet. That's a relief more than anything. I cry because he managed to find all my insecurities and pick open the scars that covered them.

DAYS AGO, I would have told you I wanted a break from work. Today, working is all I want to do. I took as many extra trips as possible while staying under regulations to get out of LA. Chet hasn't shown up at my house since Darren told him to get lost, but he has been blowing up my phone.

I blocked his number, but he still finds ways to contact me. For someone who has a day job, he sure has a lot of free time to harass me. To say he isn't taking the breakup well would be an understatement. As mad as I am that he put his hands on me, it's the kick I needed to never get back with him again.

We had been on-again-off-again for a while but are completely off now. I'm not the best at stopping men from hurting me emotionally, but physically? That's something I won't put up with. I'm embarrassed it got that far. I had to cancel dinner plans with my parents because I was nervous they might see the bruises.

I also missed a video call with Rob because as much as I love my little brother, he tends to be overprotective. He'd be able to tell something was off, and I don't need him blowing off his team to fly here and beat up Chet, no matter how satisfying that would be.

Today's extra shift means I am once again serving champagne in first class when a pair of navy eyes lock with my lighter ones. A genuine smile takes over my face for the first time in days. Ralphie gives me his best imitation of a friendly greeting until his expression morphs into something more serious—something lethal.

Peering down, I realize his gaze is locked on my wrist. The bracelets I wore to hide the bruising slid up, exposing enough of the purple marks that someone paying attention could determine what they are. When his eyes flit back up to mine and his nostrils flare, I know I won't be able to brush off this conversation with him the way I have with everyone else.

FOUR

Ralphie

TO SAY I am excited to see ocean-blue eyes watching me when I board my return flight to Los Angeles is an understatement. After a week on an island with my single and out-to-mingle teammates, watching Morgan help an older woman with her bag is a sweet sight. I have never been more thankful that the beginning of the season is near than I am after this trip. Something needs to rein these boys in.

Settling into my seat, I relish the way Morgan brightens when she sees me and can't help but admire the view. Her flight attendant uniform does nothing to distract from how stunning she is. The outfit is supposed to give them a similar appearance, but in true Morgan fashion, she personalized hers with several bracelets that shift up and down her arm as she moves.

After one movement, they slide up far enough that I notice something on her wrist. Did a pen explode? The area under her bracelets is covered in small bluish smudges. When her arm twists, a lead ball drops in my stomach, and I realize the marks make the shape of a hand around her wrist. I don't think those are from ink.

Rage swells in my chest. Her reaction when she sees where I was staring tells me everything I need to know. Someone grabbed her wrist hard enough to leave bruises. Considering I didn't notice them last week, I'm betting they are fresh and that I know exactly who marked her golden skin.

I stew in my seat through the pre-flight service, where she deftly avoids coming near me, and the safety demonstration when her focus is straight in front of her. I'm tempted to press the call button after take-off, but I suspect she would send her coworker. The fact that I can wait this patiently with the amount of fury building inside me is a testament to my time playing hockey. Without that discipline, I would have blown up already and demanded answers.

After stalling all she could, Morgan approaches my row. "Hello. What would you prefer for your in-flight meal?"

"Morgan," I say, disregarding her spiel.

"We have chicken salad or BBQ sliders. Personally, I prefer the chicken salad; the BBQ can be heavy for—"

"Morgan."

"For air travel, but your stature says you aren't afraid of a heavy meal and need as much protein as you can—"

"*Zlatíčko!*" Though quiet, my voice comes out as a command she can't ignore. When she finally flashes those baby blues down to me, they are full of trepidation. Slowly, so as not to startle her, I reach my hand over hers. Avoiding her wrist as much as I can, I move her sleeve and bracelets to better inspect the bruises.

Turning her arm, I examine the dark purple marks. "Who?" I question without glancing away from the abused area.

"It's fine. It was an accident. Someone grabbed me too tightly. It looks worse than it is."

"I've been grabbed accidentally and intentionally many times in my life, honey, by exceptionally strong men. None left marks that resembled these."

"I must bruise easily. Maybe I should have my doctor see if I'm anemic," she suggests lightly, but I can tell she's trying to diffuse my anger. Surely, she knows it isn't directed at her—never at her.

I'm not buying that explanation, and she knows it based on how she swallows when I shift my gaze back to her face. She tries to pull her arm away, but I gently run my thumb over the bruises. Normally, it is a soothing action, but seeing the marks under my motions makes my blood boil.

"Where does he live?" I ask in a fierce tone I hardly recognize.

"What? Why?"

I don't reply, but when she tugs against my hold again, I reluctantly release her arm. She sighs as she takes in my fierce expression.

"I appreciate your concern, but you don't need to worry about this."

"You handled it then? Did you file a report?"

"The police aren't going to care about a few bruises. They barely help during real domestic disputes," she chuffs.

"It seems we've come full circle then. Where can I find him, Morgan?"

"Ralphie," she sighs. "It's fine. I promise. Things got out of hand when I broke up with him, but I ended it. He isn't my problem anymore, and he sure as hell isn't yours."

As angry as I am that the prick laid his hands on her, I am happy to hear that she ended it with him. Not only because I want a chance with her but also because no woman should be with a man who hurts them.

"You broke up with him because he did that?"

"No, he did that because I broke up with him," she clarifies. "I mean, not *because*, but to stop me. It didn't work, and now he's out of my life. I'm better for it. Turns out, he was subtly manipulating to mold me into his perfect Stepford wife."

"Mold you?" I question. The Stepford reference eludes me, but I can gather enough from the context. What I don't understand is why he would need to 'mold' her. She's already perfect.

"Mhmm," she hums. "Apparently, I am 'too much' to be a good wife. I may cook a mean Shepard's Pie and give great head, but I'm still only a working-class airhead who has potential but isn't good enough as is."

And the rage is back. "He said that to you?!" I demand.

"Not in those exact words, but yes. Whatever, it doesn't matter.

He's old news. Now, do you want the sliders or the chicken salad?" I almost grin at the drop of her professional demeanor.

Sensing that I've pushed her as far as I can on this topic, I choose my lunch and let her return to work. If she thinks this is the end of the conversation, she has another thing coming. I may not be going after the douche canoe—yet—but I won't let Morgan believe the things he said about her. She may have brushed it off, but I can see the ding in her confidence since I last saw her. She'll know how incredible she is if it's the last thing I do, whether she gives me a shot or not.

Before the end of our uneventful flight, I convince her to give me her number. It's under the guise of getting on the list for Two-One-Oh, but I don't feel bad about the deceit. I do *technically* plan to go to the club and sit in her section. I just also plan to do whatever it takes to make her forget her shithead ex and know how much better she deserves to be treated.

THE REST of the week drags as I wait until Morgan works at the club. She mentioned that since she is picking up extra flights this week, she won't be there until Thursday. That's fine, though. Out of season, my schedule is wide open. All I do during the off-season is train and work on the areas I need to improve from the prior season.

Today, I'm training with Connor, Mikelson, and Danvers. Fitz would normally be here, but he is still on his honeymoon. Connor is a winger with me, while Fitz and Mikelson play defense. Danvers is our goalie. He's a bit of an odd duck, but what goalie isn't? He's the youngest of our group, but he's damn good, having the most shutouts in the Pacific Division last season.

Since we can't scrimmage, we spend most of our session working on drills, which leads to racing.

"Damn," Connor whistles. "I can't remember the last time I beat Wreck-It Ralph in a foot race."

"Shut it," I say, bumping his shoulder. "Don't get used to it. And is it considered a foot race if we are on skates?"

"Tomato, to-mah-to" he replies.

"You do seem off your game," Danvers notes.

Mikelson sighs. "D, we've been through this. Some thoughts are inside thoughts."

"I'd want to know if I was sucking," Danvers mutters.

I throw the towel I used to wipe the sweat off my forehead at him in retaliation. He shoots me a disgruntled glare.

"Don't poke the team grouch," Connor chides. I don't argue about the title. My quiet nature and sheer size intimidate most people. I revel in the grump moniker. It means most people leave me alone, and opponents think twice before squaring up.

"You good, though, bro?" my teammate asks. "Not still pining after the sexy bottle girl?"

I bristle at him regarding Morgan as simply the 'sexy bottle girl.' She is drop-dead gorgeous, but in our brief interactions and texts, I've discovered she's much more than that. Sure, she enjoys a good party, but she also spends her other evenings crocheting and binge-watching sitcoms. She has atrocious taste in music and grocery shops for her elderly neighbor, Sybil. She thinks she isn't smart, but she has more emotional intelligence than I could ever hope to possess. She is more dimensional than she lets people see, and it's their loss.

"I'm not pining for her at all," I scoff. "I'm seeing her tonight."

"No shit?" Connor asks, astonished.

"She's working at a club in Hollywood. I'd invite you fuckers to join, but I don't want to bring you down with my grouchiness."

"Whoa there," Mikelson interjects. "I never said anything. I could use a night out."

The others agree.

"I'll see if she can get you guys on the list, too," I tell them.

I shake my head as Connor and Mikelson chest bump. I cannot wait for Fitz to come home and help me deal with these miscreants.

1:12 PM

ME

Is there room for any more on tonight's list?

ZLATÍČKO

Depends… Are you bringing more hockey hunks?

ME

Does that mean you think I'm a hunk? ;)

And yes. Three, if that's okay.

ZLATÍČKO

Of course, my boss will love me for bringing in NHL customers. She is always on our asses about getting more athletes in here. She says they are 'less annoying than the artist types' and can 'put away more drinks.'

ME

We are happy to prove her right.

Be there at 11?

ZLATÍČKO

See you then! I'll be the one wearing sequins, in case you can't find me.

ME

Morgan, I'd be able to find you in a room filled with a thousand clones.

FIVE

Morgan

I NEVER THOUGHT a text with the word 'clone' in it would give me butterflies, but here I am, practically swoony over my conversation with Ralphie. Since his flight earlier this week, he has made sure to text me every day. He hasn't been outwardly flirty, which is confusing. But he has been constant. I may be reading too much into it because I low key want him to flirt with me.

Usually, I'd spend a week or two eating chocolate in bed after a breakup, but I am more glad to be rid of Chet than sad. If anything, I'm disappointed I let someone manipulate me and hurt my already fragile self-esteem.

Not wanting to kill the buzz I got from Ralphie's text, I down the rest of my cocktail. One of the things I love about Two-One-Oh is the pre-shift drinks the bartenders serve. The club doesn't have a uniform per se, but the dress code is strict. They prefer that we wear neutral color dresses, but the material is up to us, which is why I'm wearing a glittery silver number. Combined with my teased hair and bright red lips, I am projecting confidence. Fake it till you make it.

It turns out that I need every ounce of confidence my outfit gives me tonight. Not only are the hockey hunks late, but Chet and his friends somehow managed to get a table. Unlike Greg, Martina isn't lenient with freebies. This night is going to cost them a couple of grand.

I don't know what he's planning, but I don't have a good feeling about it, considering he has never wanted to drop money here before. The hate comments I've been getting on social media and texts from burner numbers tell me whatever he as planned isn't a joyful reconciliation.

Steeling myself to face him, I saunter over to his booth and plaster on my brightest, fakest smile. "Hey guys, are you all taken care of over here?"

All eyes shoot to me and then Chet. I guess he's taking the lead on this exchange. "No, actually. Service here is shit. And the help leaves a lot to be desired."

"I'm sorry to hear that," I reply. They sat down two minutes ago, but he speaks as if they've been waiting an hour. "What can we do to fix that for you?"

"If you could get us a server that isn't a gold-digging slut, that would be preferable. But if not, we'll take a bottle of Maker's, six glasses, and a round of Heinekens. Think you can handle that?"

"Of course." I nod, facade in place.

As I turn to leave, I hear him snicker at his friends. "She was always good at serving. Better when she's on—" I walk away to prevent hearing how the sentence ends. I'm not going to let him get to me tonight. That's what he wants.

Grabbing a tray, I walk up to the bar to get the items they requested. By the time I return, their section is swarming with women. Chet sits on the back couch with a girl on his lap. She's whispering in his ear, but his gaze is locked on mine. If he thought this show was going to make me jealous, he is going to be disappointed. I don't envy that girl at all.

Instead of being disappointed, Chet is mad. My lack of response to his taunting has enraged him, and he is taking it out on me. I've done more for their table than all my others combined. And I know there will be no tip at the end of it. The tips from my other tables will likely be crap, too, since I have hardly had any time for them.

The more I smile and pretend his barbs don't bother me, the redder his face gets. He wants to break me. Maybe see me cry? But it is going to take a lot more than his pompous ass hurling insults at me. He isn't saying anything I haven't heard in my head.

I can't say it doesn't hurt,to have someone I trusted treat me this way, though. A few weeks ago, I was sitting up, waiting on his texts and validation. Now, he's outwardly insulting me in front of a crowd. Half of the group has the decency to appear uncomfortable while the rest live for the drama.

Chet must finally reach his breaking point at my unaffected attitude because as I clear bottles off the table, he grabs my wrist. The same one whose faint bruises I covered in concealer. I bite my lip to hold in my hiss of pain.

"It doesn't seem you're having the best night, Morgan," he sneers. "I thought you liked serving big shots?"

I fight the urge to laugh at deeming himself a big shot. "What do you want? I'm trying to do my job."

"What I *wanted* was for you to realize your low-class skank ass was dating above your league, but for some reason, you think you're hot shit. A girl like you was lucky for everything I did to help you climb the social ladder. And you had the nerve to end things with *me*?! All the bleach in your fake-ass blonde hair must have finally given you brain damage. Maybe it's time for someone to do something about that."

Before I can ask what he means, cold liquid falls over my head, soaking my hair and chest. I stare down as the whiskey seeps into my dress, frozen in shock. Chet's cruel laugh being cut short finally draws my attention back to the world around me.

I'm surprised by the sight that greets me. Ralphie has Chet gripped by the neck as the smaller man claws at him. Three large men I recognize from the bachelor party, stand sentry, glaring at Chet's friends as if daring them to intervene. There may be more of them, but I don't like their chances, and clearly, neither do they. The girls from earlier scatter as the club's bouncers make their way over.

Realizing the optics, I step toward the entangled pair. I don't know the protocol for stopping someone from choking out someone else, but I'm pretty sure I'm not supposed to make any sudden movements. Unfortunately, time is of the essence.

"Ralphie! Let him go!"

The man in question glances at me over his shoulder. His navy eyes look black in the club lighting, but I don't miss their fury. His posture tells me he has no plans to let Chet go, but if he doesn't want to get kicked out, he needs to ASAP.

"He's not worth it," I shout over the commotion. "Let him go. I don't want you to get in trouble."

Still no movement. Alright, it's time to employ a different tactic. Approaching him slowly, I place a hand lightly on his back and lean in. "Please? I need you."

I swear the man lets out a growl before he loosens his grip. Chet crashes down to the couch, and his hands automatically go to his neck as he sucks in air. I grab Ralphie's arm to pull him away, but he leans over instead, putting the two men face to face. I roll my lips to hold in a smirk when Chet flinches. Ralphie is speaking too low for me to hear what he says, but whatever it is has the red-faced Chet paling.

He continues to stare at the man until he nods. Satisfied by whatever Chet agreed to, Ralphie turns his back to him and pushes me out of the booth. Our exit is timed perfectly with the arrival of the bouncers.

"Are you okay, Morgan?" Larson, my favorite asks.

"I'm fine," I confirm. "It takes more than a few unruly customers to mess with me. Luckily, the big guy here saved the day."

"He didn't give you any trouble?" the other bouncer asks dubiously, surveying my now disheveled appearance thanks to Chet's whiskey shower. Ralphie lets out a grumble of dissent.

"No, he saved me. I think it's time Mr. Daniels went home, though," I say, sparing Chet a glance as his friends surround him.

"He's leaving," Ralphie booms from beside me. "As are you," he directs my way.

My two coworkers look between us and at each other before shrugging. "We'll help him find the door."

Without waiting to watch them leave, Ralphie pulls me toward the back of the club. "What are you doing? I can't leave now. I'm only halfway through my shift."

He doesn't reply as he gently drags me to the 'Employees Only' door. "Put in the code."

"I'm not putting in the code," I state with a stomp of my foot. "I can't leave."

"Are you planning to work the rest of your shift sticky and smelling like a distillery?"

Sighing, I realize he is right. If I want to stay, I need to clean up. I can't walk around covered in liquor. After I type in the code, Ralphie ushers me through the back, poking his head through doors as we pass.

"It's the one at the end of the hall," I say before he searches every closet. When we get to the dressing room, he walks in behind me and shuts the door. Whipping around, I level him with my harshest glare.

It's time Mr. Hockey Hunk and I have a chat.

SIX

Ralphie

DESPITE MY STAUNCH REFUSAL, the guys convinced me we needed to get dinner before going to the club. Dinner turned into 'pre-drinks,' which turned into us getting to Two-One-Oh over an hour after we were supposed to. Our tardiness meant we were given the last available booth and Cherri as a server.

I asked her several times to tell Morgan we were here, but she either didn't relay the message or Morgan was mad at me for being late and ignoring us. I'm not sure which I would prefer.

"Oh my God," Mikelson groans. "If you sigh one more time, I am going to assume a thirteen-year-old girl has replaced the great Radek Nokavik." I glare at him over my beer.

"Leave the man alone," Connor defends. "His girl hasn't come over yet."

"She's not my girl," Danvers corrects.

"She will be. She broke up with the Tanger Outlet Twit, right?"

"Yes," I confirm. Thoughts of Morgan's ex fill me with rage when I remember the marks he left on her delicate skin.

"Then you're halfway there. You just have to make your move in a way that is classy and not creepy."

"Why would it come off creepy?" I ask.

"Because she recently ended a relationship," Danvers chimes in. "She might think you're hoping to be her rebound and fuck her through the sadness."

"Not helpful, D," Connor comments as I scowl at our teammate.

"Come on, man. Let's make the rounds and see if we can spot her in the crowd. I think our server is too preoccupied trying to catch Mikelson's eye to risk Morgan taking our table away."

The two of us get up and move toward the center of the VIP area.

"I don't want to be a rebound," I assert as I search the crowd.

"Then show her you're more than rebound material."

"How?"

"How do you feel about playing knight in shining armor?" he asks, full of concern. I shift my gaze to see what caught his attention. Across the room stands Morgan, dripping in amber liquid, while her soon-to-be-dead ex laughs, bottle in hand.

I sense Connor speaking beside me, but all I can hear is the blood rushing between my ears. Pushing through the crowd, I stomp over to the douche who dared fuck with such a sweet soul. It will be the last time he does if I have anything to say about it.

Brushing past his friends, I grab Chet by his throat and pin him against the wall. His uncalloused hands slap at mine, but my grip is firm. I'm not a fighter. My specialty is busting through coverage and leaving it behind, not confronting it. Almost every punch I've thrown has been in defense of myself or a teammate. My ability to stay composed is well-known and hated throughout the league. Tonight, though, I'm ready to throw it all away. Something about Morgan has all that control going out the window.

Tightening my grasp on his neck, I watch the panic flare in Chet's eyes with satisfaction and wonder if this is how he felt when he was tormenting Morgan. Doubt it. The pain I'm causing is for noble reasons. His was to assuage his overgrown ego. I'm not holding tight enough to make him pass out, but it is enough to make taking in air a challenge.

I don't know how long I stand there watching him struggle when I hear Morgan's melodic voice beside me.

"Ralphie," she calls. She doesn't know this, but I love that her mouth isn't sullied by using my real name. A name given to me by a deadbeat who doesn't deserve to be considered a father after he deserted my mother with four young kids. I much prefer her to know me as Ralphie, the hockey player, than Radek, the boy hustling to make it out while watching out for my mom and sisters.

She pleads with me to release the scumbag, but I'm not ready yet. I'm still struggling to reign in my rage. It isn't until I hear her say she needs me that I give in and let him drop onto the couch.

The heat of her hand on my back sears me, but I have a message to deliver. Looming over Chet, I make sure this never happens again.

"Listen closely, you sniveling swine. If you ever touch, call, or even breathe in the same zip code as Morgan again, you're going to wish you hadn't. I didn't live through the dissolution of my country without learning how to make someone disappear without a trace. If you don't want your family plastering your face on a milk carton, you will never cross my path or hers again. Understand?"

It's a bluff. I may have lived in poverty, but I didn't do anything dangerous growing up. In fact, I mostly worked my ass off to be good enough to play hockey overseas. He doesn't know that, though. And my posturing works as he pales in front of me. Slowly, he nods his head. With his confirmation, I turn my back to him and usher Morgan out of the booth and away from the waste of space.

I didn't notice my teammates joining the fray, but it explains why none of the jerkwad's friends stepped in to help him. They post up beside me as the club's bouncers arrive to assess the situation. I almost snap when one of them touches Morgan, but she diffuses the situation, and they head off to deal with Chet.

Pulling my girl in the other direction, I search for the employee lounge where she can clean up before we leave. She fights me at first, but when I point out she can't keep working covered in whiskey, she leads me inside a room in the back. The way she stomped her foot in protest was so fucking adorable that I had to stop myself from kissing her right then.

When I follow her into a dressing room, she appears surprised before a stern expression crosses her face.

"Just because you played hero doesn't mean you get to boss me around. This is my workplace. I can't leave. I appreciate what you did for me. It was sweet and, honestly, hella hot. Chet deserved what he got, but I have tables. Martina isn't going to be cool with me disappearing in the middle of my shift. I'll clean up as best I can and finish the night."

"No," I say.

"No?"

"No."

"You can't tell me 'no.' Unless you became the owner of this club in the last hour, you don't have a say over my schedule."

For a brief second, I wonder how much it would cost to buy Two-One-Oh. My accountant has been nagging me to diversify. My agent would love the publicity of it and cut of the profits.

"Hey," she snaps. "Are you listening to me?"

My sweet girl is riled up. Her system is processing multiple emotions after everything that's happened, which is all the more reason for her to go home.

"*Zlatíčko*," I croon. "You were assaulted. I'm sure your boss doesn't expect you to finish out the night."

"You've never met Martina."

When my phone vibrates in my pocket, I slide it out and read the message. "I have not, but Connor has."

"What?" Her head tilts in confusion, causing a drop of whiskey to fall onto the top of her chest. What I wouldn't give to follow it with my tongue.

Now isn't the time to be thinking sexy thoughts. I need to focus on taking care of Morgan, not objectifying her.

"Connor—the guy who planned Fitz's bachelor party —talked to your boss, and she said it would be fine if you went home. In fact, she insists."

"Why?" The puzzled expression on her face beckons for my kiss. Still, I hold off.

"Is she firing me?!"

"Of course not. Connor can be very persuasive. And as the team's unofficial event planner, he probably mentioned the team stopping by here more often."

"Oh."

"Yeah, oh." I smirk.

Instead of moving, Morgan closes her eyes and inhales deeply. I silently watch her collect herself.

"I'm afraid to look in the mirror," she whispers. My chest tightens at the admission, and I pull her into my arms.

She melts into my hold until she suddenly pushes against my chest. "You're going to ruin your shirt. I'm all sticky and wet."

"I like you sticky and wet," I reply as I let her go. She shakes her head at me, but a smile graces her lips for the first time since the Chet ordeal.

"Thank you again for what you did out there. You didn't have to."

I grunt at that. Of course, I did. I would have stepped into the situation regardless of what woman was being harrassed. I probably wouldn't have choked and threatened to disappear the offender had it been someone else, but I would have done something.

"I should change," she notes. "I'm sorry I didn't see you guys much tonight. You'll have to come back another day."

"Tomorrow."

"Tomorrow? I don't work tomorrow."

"You'll see me tomorrow when I take you to dinner."

"To dinner?" She repeats, puzzled. "You mean a late-night bite?"

"You said you don't work tomorrow."

"I don't."

"Are you busy at seven?"

"No."

"Then why would we eat dinner later?"

Morgan flushes, and her hands pick at the sequins on her dress. "I don't know. That is usually when people go out."

"People?" I muse out loud. Then it clicks. Morgan is used to dating assholes like the one who harassed her earlier. Guys that aren't interested in getting to know a woman—at least not clothed. They grab drinks or quick bites to get to the 'fun' part of the evening as fast as possible. I wonder when she was last taken on a proper date.

"'People' may eat dinner late, but I don't. I eat at the normal time, and I want you to join me. Is that something you want, too?"

Blinking at me, she nods.

"Good," I reply. Finally giving into the urge I've been fighting all night, I run my hand against her cheek down to her chin. Tilting her head up, I lean down and meet her for a kiss. It's not a passionate, life-changing kiss. But the chaste meeting of our lips is powerful nonetheless. With a quick peck to her forehead, I back out of the room and leave her to change.

When I return to the main area, Danvers and Mikelson chat with Cherri and another server. Connor passes me a fresh beer. "She okay?"

"She will be," I answer.

"Did you ask her out?"

Taking a sip from my beer, I don't reply. But the tip of my lips must tell him everything he needs to know because he shakes his head and grins. Downing the rest of his drink, he slaps me on the shoulder. "I'm going to go save Mikelson's chances of scoring. I assume you want to leave now that she's gone?"

He chuckles when I nod. As he grabs Danvers and checks that our other teammate can find his own way home, I rack my brain for the perfect place to take Morgan tomorrow.

SEVEN

Morgan

WHEN THE NEXT afternoon rolls around, I am freaking the fuck out. Ralphie has given me approximately zero information on where he is taking me except that it's casual, and I can 'wear anything.' Unhelpful brute. Doesn't he know getting ready for a date, especially a first date, takes hours of preparation and thought?

Not that I have been on many recently. I'd hardly call what Chet and I did dating. He tended to call them 'outings,' which is one of the reasons I was surprised by his attempts to label our relationship.

After trying on everything in my closet, I debate sending Ralphie another text. He seems to value directness, but I also don't want to come off as needy before whatever this is has a chance to blossom. Part of me thinks he pities me over what happened and is taking me out to make up for it. A larger, unacknowledged part hopes that isn't what this is and that he wants to date me. I know better than to listen to that part, though. Girls like me don't end up with sexy, hot-shot pro athletes.

"Whoa," I hear from behind me as I primp in the mirror. "Did a Forever 21 explode in here?"

"I know," I groan to Madison. "I have no idea what to wear on this date!"

"Where is he taking you?"

"He won't tell me."

"Where are you meeting him?"

"I'm not."

"What do you mean?" she questions with a tilt of her head.

"He's coming to pick me up," I reply.

"Wow. I can't remember the last time a first date picked me up. I can't remember the last time my *boyfriend* picked me up." Bitterness tinges her admission. Madison picks men about as well as I do. Something we have commiserated the few times we've found each other on the couch drowning our sorrows.

"Yeah, I thought it was strange, too. He'll be here soon, and I have nothing to wear."

"Hold that thought." Madison leaves my room before returning a few minutes later with a blue off-the-shoulder dress. Thankfully, she is a similar height to me, so it isn't too short.

"This is perfect," I squeal as I pull her into a hug. Not the most physically affectionate person, she freezes for a moment before returning the gesture.

"Okay," she says as she pulls away, "save the touchy-feely stuff for your date."

"I'm not sure how touchy-feely it will be. I haven't found any PDA pictures of him. Since he was adamant about going out this early, I don't think he'll want to risk it. He doesn't exactly strike me as a hand holder anyway."

"You never know. I'll let you finish getting ready."

Thanking her again, I touch up my hair and apply a shiny, pink gloss. I went for a natural makeup look, but it takes almost as many products to achieve as my glam looks do. At seven on the dot, I hear a loud knock as I tie the straps of my wedges.

Opening the door, I practically drool at the sight before me. Ralphie is dressed more casually than I've seen before in a white polo and navy shorts. I try not to fidget at the heat in his gaze as he takes me in.

"Hi," I breathe.

"Hello, *Zlatíčko*. You are a vision."

"Thank you. Is this okay for what we're doing?" I twirl around so he gets the full effect of my outfit.

"The dress is perfect, but you may want different shoes. We will be walking a decent amount."

"I could walk miles in these," I scoff. He eyes me skeptically.

"I'll change into something more comfortable, though." The slight lift to his lips makes the change of footwear worth it.

Now in Keds, I saunter out of my bedroom and join him back in the entry. "Better?"

He nods, opening the door for me to walk out in front of him. It's easy to guess which car in the parking lot is his. It's not that his luxury SUV is flashy, but it is way more expensive than anything else around despite its sensibility.

When we approach it, my hand lands on top of his on the handle. Shooting him a puzzled expression, I remove mine, allowing him to open the door. As he lets me get situated, he leans slightly into my space.

"When we're out together, don't expect to touch any doors." I mull over his declaration as he walks around the car, I wonder where this man came from and how I can keep him here.

THROUGHOUT THE RIDE, we make idle small talk, which is really me talking with the occasional interjection from him, usually in response to a direct question. Wherever he is taking me isn't too far from my apartment because, after fifteen minutes, he is pulling into a parking lot in Santa Monica. Glancing around, I see people milling about on a blocked-off street.

"Are you going to tell me what we're doing now?"

"You'll see," he replies with a smirk. When I reach for my door handle, he makes a disapproving grunt. I guess he plans to open it so I can get in *and* out. With a sigh, I wait for him to come around and take his help climbing down from his SUV. While I may pretend I find it silly and unnecessary, I'm swooning inside.

Ralphie leads us toward the cordoned-off area, and that's when the sights and sounds hit me. It's a street fair! Stalls are set up on either side of the road, where vendors sell goods and food. As we get closer, I can read the banner at the top: *Santa Monica Crafts Fair*.

"You brought me to a crafts fair?" I ask, a lump caught in my throat.

Cataloging my features, I see doubt creep into his expression. "Is that okay? If you don't want to go, we can do something else. I figured you might be interested in this since you like to crochet." The uncertainty in his voice, combined with his accent, melts me almost as much as the gesture.

I expected him to take me to dinner at a swanky restaurant or maybe to a publicity event. I didn't expect him to plan a date that catered to my interests. Interests I don't openly talk about to many people.

Placing my hand on his arm, I squeeze to reassure him as much as to ground myself. "It's perfect."

Ralphie gives me a self-satisfied nod before turning back to the fair. He allows the hand on his arm to slide down before he grabs it and interlocks our fingers. I guess I was wrong about him being the hand-holding type.

We walk silently, surveying everything before I am drawn into a stall called *Handmade Jewelry by Tina*. Looking at the delicate pieces, I smile at the owner.

"These are beautiful."

"Thank you," she replies in kind. "Are you searching for anything particular?"

"We're just browsing. I don't know much about crystals," I reply sheepishly.

"When is your birth month?"

"June."

"That's a good one. Moonstone," she says as she searches around her stall.

"I thought my birthstone was a pearl?"

"It is. But your birth crystal is often recognized as a moonstone. It symbolizes new beginnings, good fortune, and inner peace."

I glance over to see what Ralphie thinks of this. I doubt he buys into 'hippie mumbo jumbo,' as my dad would call it. But I see nothing but neutral expression reflected at me.

"Ah ha! This one," Tina exclaims. In her hands, she has a short necklace made of tiny diamond-shaped whitish stones. When she fastens it behind my neck, it sits at the base. She holds up a mirror for me to see once it is secure.

"Wow, it's gorgeous," I mutter.

"It looks good on you," Ralphie replies.

"How much—" The question halts on my tongue as I see Ralphie pass several bills to Tina.

"What are you doing?" I question.

"Buying the necklace," he states matter-of-factly.

"I was going to pay for it."

"And I did instead. The result is the same," he retorts as if buying me jewelry on a first date is normal. It isn't expensive, but it's still jewelry. On a first date.

"Did you see anything else you wanted?"

"Why? Are you going to buy that, too?"

The expression he gives me says that, obviously, yes, he was.

"I'm good for now. I'm actually kind of hungry."

Waving bye to Tina, we head to the section of the fair where most of the food trucks are set up. Surveying the offerings, I get lost in my head until my eyes meet Ralphie's. He's watching me as if I'm the most interesting thing here.

"Tacos?" I suggest.

Ralphie nods and leads us to the Mexican truck nearby. After placing our order and fielding a glare when I tried to pay for dinner, we grab our food and sit at a table. Eating my fish tacos as daintily as I can, I watch Ralphie scarf down his steak carnitas.

"You're from the Czech Republic originally?" I ask as if I didn't Google him at least four times already.

"Yes, I lived there until I was eighteen and then came to the US to play hockey."

"Do you go home often?"

"No, my time spent there was not the best. I send money back to my mother and sisters but haven't been back since I moved. Home is here now."

"You aren't close with your family?"

He shrugs. Needing to fill the silence, I tell him about my family and how my parents had me young. I detail how close my little brother and I are despite begging my parents to exchange him for a girl when they first brought him home from the hospital.

"He was drafted recently, right?"

"Yes! He was picked up by Seattle in the first round. I'm so proud of him. He has been working toward this goal forever. When all the other kids were drawing in the dirt during Little League, he was testing out bats to find out which one helped him hit the best. I'm surprised you remember that. He was drafted the night of your friend's bachelor party. There was a lot going on." I muse.

"Of course, I remember. You beamed every time you mentioned it."

I blush at his assessment as I recall that night. I may have brought it up a couple times. In my defense, they're professional athletes so they understand the unique pressure. I hope Rob find a group of teammates to support him the way they seem to.

"It's nice you have such close friends here since your family is far away. I've lived here my entire life and don't have a bond with anyone the way you all seem to."

He snorts, but his face softens at my wistful tone. "We're as close as a bunch of men who spend three-fourths of the year together can be. If you asked most of them, they would probably say they don't know me that well."

"Why is that?"

"Hockey has always been serious to me. It was a way out of poverty and into a new life. I don't take it as lightly as many of the American players do, which can make me come off as a hard ass. My agent, Andre, would tell you it's because I'm a grumpy asshole.

Coming from a similar background to me, he understands my mindset."

"I don't think you're an asshole. If anything, I would call you quiet but sweet. It's okay to be serious; I should be more that way."

"You are perfect the way you are," he states firmly. "And I am only sweet to you. If you told the guys or Andre that I was sweet, I am not sure they would believe you."

My cheeks heat at his compliment. There is something endearing about his words being both gruff and gentle. Embarrassed by my reaction, I quickly change the subject. "Do you miss anything from home?"

"I miss some of the food."

"But we have tacos," I tease, wiggling mine at him.

"You do have tacos," he laughs with a gleam in his eyes.

"What food do you miss the most?"

"Do you want to see?"

"Like a picture?" He shakes his head.

"There is a truck over there that serves kolaches. They were my favorite as a child."

"What is a kolache?"

"There are many kinds. It is delicious filling surrounded by pastry. Sweet ones are filled with fruit or cheese and savory with sausage. The savory ones are not as authentic but make for a great breakfast."

As we saddle up to the truck, I notice several flavors that sound yummy. "What's the best kind?"

"My favorite is apricot or cream cheese. It all depends on what fruit you like."

I choose a blueberry and cream cheese mixture while Ralphie orders apricot.

"These are incredible," I say over a mouthful.

"I'm glad you enjoy them. The truck owners opened a cafe near my house last month. I'm afraid the team nutritionist will have my head with how many I've eaten this off-season."

"That's lucky," I muse.

"I wouldn't say it's luck as much as choosing a location near their biggest investor."

"Is that investor you?" He shrugs in response, and I can't stop the giggle that spills out of me. It's cute that a this two-hundred-and-thirty pound polar bear of a man can still be shy.

"Come on. We have more of booths left to check out. Don't think I missed you eyeing the one full of yarn."

We finish the pastries and continue walking around the fair, stopping at a few stalls. When Ralphie is distracted at a wood carving display, I splurge on a set of hand-carved crocheting hooks. He sends me an unimpressed glare but doesn't say anything when he spots my bag.

After we've made a few laps, Ralphie drives me home. Walking me to the door, he kisses my forehead before listening to me lock up behind me.

It's only 10 p.m., and I'm perplexed. On one hand, I appreciate him showing me that he wants to spend time with me for more than my body. On the other hand, I want *his* body. He must be old-school and waiting until date number three.

EIGHT

Morgan

"I HAD A GREAT TIME, *ZLATÍČKO*," Ralphie says as we stand outside my apartment after another wonderful date. He took me to a screening of one of my favorite movies in the park tonight. That would have been sweet enough, but he also brought an honest-to-God picnic for us to eat while enjoying the show. His charcuterie skills could use some work, but the thought behind it was unmatched.

I am more than ready to show him how much I appreciate his effort, but he is once again dropping me off at my door and refusing my offer to come in.

"I have an early workout tomorrow. Maybe we can get together on Sunday? I know you have a busy week flying out tomorrow and working at the club Saturday."

Ugh. He's even understanding about my schedule. He's going to have to stop being this nice and compassionate if he isn't going to let me jump his bones.

"That works," I answer quietly, not meeting his gaze.

His knuckle tips my chin back until we're peering into each other's eyes. I expect to see apathy, but a zing of electricity and lust zaps through my body when I spot heat. Maybe I was reading this wrong and he does want more than a quick peck tonight.

The finger on my chin moves upward to trace my cheek before his hand slips behind my head, and he pulls me toward him. Ralphie opens his mouth as if to say something but shuts it before any words come out. Instead, he presses his lips to mine softly, too softly for the inferno raging inside me.

Deciding to take what I want, I move into him until my chest is pressed against his and lick the seam of his lips. After a moment of hesitation, he opens for me and our soft kiss turns passionate. His contentment to let me lead lasts about two seconds before he takes back control, not that I mind.

The hand in my hair tightens as he devours my mouth. His other hand lands on my hip, fingers teasing the top of my ass cheek. A tidal wave of longing surges through me, and I moan into his mouth. The action shakes him from the moment, and he pulls back, chest heaving.

"Fuck, you're delectable, Morgan."

"I taste better the further down you go," I tease. I wouldn't usually say something that forward, but the way his nostrils flare erases any shyness.

"I have no doubt," he mutters, almost to himself. "I can't wait to find out for myself."

I clench my thighs at the prospect, but when I turn to unlock my door, he stops me. "I'll see you Sunday."

I study his face, searching to understand the change in mood, but I don't find anything. I can see the hunger in his eyes and the bulge in his shorts. For whatever reason, he isn't letting himself have me yet. Maybe he isn't as ready to commit as I thought. He seems the type of guy who wouldn't want me to get too attached before we lay down ground rules. I've heard that speech a million times. I know how it goes.

I want to tell him that, but something stops me. I think hearing Ralphie say he doesn't want anything serious would crush me in a way I'm not prepared for. Instead of replying out loud, I nod and accept his peck on my forehead.

Flopping down on my bed, I replay the night in my head. It was a perfect date. We ate. We talked about our weekends. We laughed. Well, I laughed. He's more of a chuckle on the inside guy, but I heard a few chuffs during the movie.

Now that I think about it, I did dominate the conversation and knocked over my wine after a giggling fit. In my defense, you can't *not* laugh at Melissa McCarthy seducing an Air Marshal. A few people did turn to stare at us, though.

Rubbing my hands down my face, I realize I was a bit full-on tonight. I also shouldn't have worn wedges and a silk skirt to the park. It wasn't the most practical for sitting on a blanket and side-eye from the other attendees tells me I looked out of place.

Ralphie is a low-profile guy. He doesn't enjoy attention. I bet he was uncomfortable by the stares I drew. He asked me out for another date and kissed me goodnight, though. That has to count for something.

Letting out a frustrated huff, I wash off my makeup and prepare for bed. A good night's sleep will hopefully make my head more clear.

I WAKE up the next morning with no more clarity than the night before, and all the giddiness from the kiss gone. As much as I want to lay in bed and overanalyze our interactions, I need coffee.

As my cup brews, I scroll through social media and check out the stories I posted last night. I made sure not to post anything of Ralphie, but I *may* have soft-launched him a tiny bit with his legs in the frame. He doesn't have any tattoos or identifying features, so it isn't as if anyone but me will know or notice.

Scratch that. One person will notice. And she's calling me right now.

"Hi, Tini Rini," I greet my brother's girlfriend. "How is my future sister-in-law?"

"You can't call me that. We are not engaged. I still have two years of college left."

"Semantics, my dear Carina. Rob is crazy about you. It will happen."

"We'll see. Stop distracting me. I didn't call to chat about myself. I called to talk about the mystery man in last night's story."

"What mystery man?"

"You know exactly who I am talking about. Spill!"

"There is nothing to spill. I went out on a date with a man, and his legs happened to be in the frame of my picture."

"Liar. We both know nothing is in the frame that you don't want. How long have y'all been seeing each other? What's his name? When will he get a hard launch? Does Robby know?"

I spend the next few minutes detailing my history with Ralphie and discussing the dates we've been on. Aside from the crafts fair and movie in the park, he also took me to lunch before I left for a flight this last week at a cute cafe near the Marina.

"We're keeping it casual," I finish.

"Casual? Nothing about that story sounds casual for you or him."

"It's not as if we're exclusive or anything. We haven't even had sex. Everyone knows you can't be serious or exclusive before you've sealed the deal."

"Sealed the deal?" She makes a gagging sound.

"I don't think you have room to be grossed out, considering I caught you and my brother getting busy under the pier at his graduation party."

"We were not getting busy!" she gasps. "It was a quick make-out with some light petting."

"Carina! That is worse than 'seal the deal.' And my brother is involved. Can we not?"

She laughs. "Sorry. My point is that not everyone has the same opinion on what requirements must be met to be considered exclusive. Robby and I were exclusive before we had sex."

"Oh, my sweet angel baby," I coo. "The men in my world do. Trust me. I learned this lesson the hard way on more than one occasion. If he hasn't said it specifically, he's dating other women. And no man is locking it down without sampling the goods."

It took three different men asking me why I thought we were exclusive to get that point, but I keep that to myself. Rob is, thankfully, a much more noble man than the men I date. It helps that he and Carina are college sweethearts, and she was a virgin when they got together. The rules are different. I don't remind her of any of those points, though.

"If that's the case, are you seeing anyone else then?" she inquires, knowing that isn't how I roll. I always get too attached too soon and can never play the game. That's why I always end up crying into a tub of Ben and Jerry's that I've had longer than the man who broke my heart.

"Not really. I've talked to a few guys on dating apps, but nothing has made it into the real world."

"Let me know if that changes," she requests. "Your brother is calling me before his practice. I have to go. Text me when you have updates!"

"You got it, sis. Tell my loser brother to text me back."

"Will do!"

My mood lifts after talking to Carina, but I am still unsettled by everything. If I could choose Ralphie, I would. But I don't want to put all my eggs in one basket. I've made that mistake too many times. The idea of seeing anyone else makes my stomach churn, but I vow to think it over.

MY PLAN TO branch out in my dating life would be a lot easier if Ralphie weren't the most confusing person in the world. Despite being busy with his preseason conditioning and my being out of pocket on five flights—including a deadhead to Little Rock—he's made time to connect.

I have been extra cautious not to come on too strong since I don't know where we stand. The same cannot be said for him. Every morning, I wake up to a text from him, and we exchange several more throughout the day, always initiated by him. He even double-texts with random thoughts or additional information when I take too long to respond. It's as if he doesn't care about the texting rules at all.

When I landed in Nashville after flight number three, he had food delivered from a restaurant he discovered during his playoff series there last year. I tried to tell him I had a per diem when I was on assignment, but that was the one text he ignored.

I can't tell if he's attempting to woo me because he thinks he has to —he doesn't—or if he's building me up because he has a weird fetish, and that is why he's waiting. He's lulling me into a false sense of security until I feel too guilty to turn him down. Maybe he has a latex kink or is building a harem.

Sweet as they are, his gestures have me more confused. Cherri offered to set me up with a friend of her brother's when I told her Ralphie and I hadn't defined our relationship. Apparently, he's been interested in me for a while and doesn't want to miss his shot now that I am 'unattached' again.

On one hand, it feels as if I would be cheating on Ralphie. But on the other, for all I know, I am one of the many women he's keeping on the line until he's ready to reveal his hockey harem plan. I don't really think he's planning a harem, but who can tell? His gruff exterior makes him impossible to read.

I desperately want to ask him what we are or where this is going, but then I would be the needy girl other guys have accused me of being. Hell, practically-peed-a-circle-around-me, Chet didn't want to put a label on things until Ralphie showed up.

I return to LA tomorrow and work a shift at Clamatis with Cherri. She's been talking to Ralphie's teammate. Hopefully, she will have some insider information on Ralphie's deal. If not, maybe I'll let her set me up. As much as I like Ralphie, I'm eager to be with someone ready to be with me, and I don't know if he is.

NINE

Ralphie

"DUDE, WHAT IS UP WITH YOU?" Fitz asks, plopping beside me on the couch.

I say nothing as I slide my phone back into my pocket. I hoped to catch Morgan before she had to work at the club tonight, but Fitz complained he hadn't seen us since his wedding and demanded we all hang out at his place. I think he's lonely because it's Tabby's first day back at the hospital.

"You're surlier than usual. Is your neighbor complaining about your hedges again?"

"No." Once my neighbor saw who owned the house he was leaving passive-aggressive notes at, they magically stopped appearing.

"Don't mind him," Connor remarks, handing me another beer. "He's extra grumpy because his girl is working tonight and can only text on breaks."

Fitz chokes on his drink before staring at me with an expression of utter betrayal.

"Your girl?!" he shouts. "I go away for a few weeks and come back to my practically celibate best friend in a relationship?"

"I was not celibate," I scoff. "Just because I keep my business to myself doesn't mean I'm not handling it."

His disgruntled expression at finding out I have had women in my life he didn't know about—not that there were many—is laughable. Almost.

Since arriving in LA, I have had a few friends-with-benefits situations, mostly with industry types who also wanted a release without all the media hoopla. It was no one's business but ours. It's different with Morgan, though.

I've never been one to wax poetic, but I want every man to know she's mine. There is a primal urge within me that wants to make her off-limits to the entire world. Instead of saying that, I simply shrug.

"Who is she?" Fitz demands.

Connor answers for me. "Remember the blonde bottle girl from your bachelor party he couldn't stop staring at?"

"She's more than a 'bottle girl.'" I glare at him. "But yes, her."

"I can't believe you didn't tell me," Fitz grumbles petulantly.

"My bad. Should I have interrupted your honeymoon to giggle on the phone about it? Want me to add you to my calendar? Then you can see when I go on dates."

"You put them on a calendar?" Danvers questions.

"No," I quip, over this conversation. When I shoot Mikelson a glance to commiserate on the idiocy of our friends, he's wearing a pensive expression.

"What?" I ask.

"What, what?" he responds.

"What's wrong with your face?"

"That isn't nice," Connor chides with a slap to my arm. "He can't help how many times his formerly pretty face has been hit on the ice."

"He could stop talking so much shit," Fitz suggests making us all chuckle.

"Not his fucked up nose," I say. "The weird expression he had when we were talking about Morgan."

"It's nothing, man. Not my business," Mikelson responds.

"It sure as fuck sounds like it's mine," I snap. He searches the group for support, but they're all watching him expectantly, even Danvers.

"Fuck it. Fine. Does Morgan know she's *your* girl? That you are exclusive?"

"Of course," I answer.

"You two defined your relationship and talked about it?"

"Not in as many words, but she knows. We've been out several times already."

"Have you talked about it? Slept together? Spent the night?"

"Who are you, TMZ? What does it matter?"

"Do you have a reason to believe she doesn't think they're exclusive?" Fitz asks, reading between the lines.

"Nothing concrete, but Cherri may have mentioned setting up Morgan with one of her brother's friends."

"What?" I roar. "Your girl is setting mine up with someone else? What the fuck?"

"Mikelson has a girl, too?!" Fitz exclaims, focusing on the wrong detail.

"It's not like that," the traitor replies. "We're keeping it casual, as Morgan assumes she and Nokavik are."

"Why would she assume that?" My head is spinning as it dissects every interaction over the last few weeks. I never explicitly told her I wanted to be exclusive, but I thought it was obvious. I text her every day. We talk about everything under the sun, and if that kiss the other night is any indication, our chemistry is off the charts.

"I don't understand. I haven't treated her as if she's casual. We haven't even had sex yet because I want her to know I think of her as more than a hookup."

I am greeted by a chorus of "ohhhs."

"She probably thinks you aren't interested, dude," Connor says. "A girl like her is used to men leading with sex. No sex equals no interest."

"What the fuck is that supposed to mean?" I grit out, not liking the implications he's making about Morgan.

"He doesn't mean anything by it," Fitz quickly explains. "He's simply pointing out that this is LA, and based on the J. Crew-reject she was dating, she is used to less honorable men than you. It's giving her mixed messages. Women assume men are less interested than they are while men assume the opposite."

Huh. That makes sense. "So she thinks that I don't want her because I'm *not* treating her badly? That because I haven't fucked her, I must not be interested in her and she should find someone who is?"

My agitation is growing the longer this conversation continues. My chest is so tight, I am afraid it's going to squeeze my heart until it bursts. The pang of guilt that Morgan thinks I don't want her is only overshadowed by rage at anyone else who thinks they can touch her.

"No," Fitz answers. "But since you haven't made your intentions clear, I'm sure she doesn't want to get her hopes up that you want something serious. Come on, man. You're on your way to being in the Hockey Hall of Fame. Only a very confident or foolish woman would presume to be in your league."

"She's not in my league. She's way above it."

"Then there is only one thing to do," Connor declares, downing the rest of his beer. "Let's go get your girl."

AFTER AN HOUR IN LA TRAFFIC, we're finally bypassing the line at Clamatis. It's packed, but Mikelson was able to reserve the last VIP booth thanks to Cherri, who also works here. The guys head to our table while I make a beeline to the stunning girl in the shiny black romper.

The dazzling grin that spreads across her face stops me in my tracks momentarily as I drink her in. When she breaks the spell to pass drinks to the table in front of her, I remember my mission and stomp forward.

"We need to talk," I say when I'm close enough for her to hear me. The smile that covers her face falls as the brightness in her eyes dims incrementally. I want to kick myself for taking away part of her shine, but I am too worked up to apologize right now. She nods her head and leads me to a back hallway into an employee bathroom.

"Couldn't wait until tomorrow to see me?" she teases, but there is a vulnerability in her tone that lets through her discomfort. I hate that she doubts my desire to see her, but I am about to change that.

I step toward her until she is backed against the tile wall of the bathroom. "No. I couldn't wait. The guys pointed out tonight that there could be a misunderstanding on your end about what is happening between the two of us."

"'What's happening,'" she repeats.

I watch her swallow, wanting to kiss down her throat. Instead of fighting the instinct, I sink my hand into her hair and tip her head to the side to gain better access. I shove my knee between her legs, pinning her to the wall with my body.

"Mhmm," I hum, running my nose against her delicate flesh. "It seems you may think this thing between us is casual."

"It's not?" Her hands move to fist my shirt to ground her no doubt. I lightly bite on her tendon in reprimand of her question before soothing the mark with my tongue.

"No, *Zlatičko*. What's happening here is so official, it needs its own tux." My mouth trails up to her ear as I continue to correct her misconceptions. "I apologize if my attempts to be a gentleman didn't make my intentions clear. Let me do that now."

I push back and tilt her head until we are eye to eye. "I want you. I want this. Officially, exclusively, whatever the fuck I need to say as long as it means you are mine and no one else's. Do you understand?"

Her lusty but befuddled expression tells me she does not. "You want to fuck me?"

"I want to fuck you until you forget the name of every other man you've ever met, let alone slept with. But I also want you. To hold you. To date you. To fight with you. To listen to you talk about those ridiculous Housewives who pretend to be friends despite hating each other. I want all of you all the time."

"I'm a lot," she whispers, spearing me again with her vulnerability.

"Good, 'cause I'll never be able to get enough," I reply against her lips. I take advantage of her intake of air to plunge my tongue into her mouth and ravage her with a kiss. I use the hand still in her hair to keep her exactly where I want her and claim her with my mouth. It takes a second, but she melts into my hold, her tongue meeting mine stroke for stroke but never fighting for dominance. If our last kiss was an exploration, this one is a possession. I groan against her lips when she unknowingly bucks her hips against my thigh, seeking friction.

When I break the kiss, pressing my forehead to hers. I see need swimming in her eyes that mirrors mine. "I want you."

"Yes," she mutters, making me laugh.

"But I'm not fucking you for the first time in a bathroom when you still have three hours left in your shift."

She whines at my statement. And the sound goes straight to my dick.

"You need me, baby?"

"Yes. That kiss was…" her confession trails off.

"Get used to it." I smirk as her legs clench tighter around mine. I retake her mouth with less vigor but no less conviction. I smile into it as she grinds against my thigh in earnest.

"Did my declaration get you hot and bothered, Morgan? You need something?"

"Yes, you."

"Can't have me right now," I reply, pressing my leg into her harder and shifting the angle. The heat from her core sears me through my jeans.

"If you were wearing a dress," I say between kisses, "I could finger your sweet little pussy until you came for me. Or I could drop to my knees and let you ride my face."

"That, let's do that."

"This sexy little number you're wearing is too tight for that."

"Take it off," she insists, attempting to push me back and remove the offending garment.

"Stop," I groan, and her eyes shoot to mine. Instead of giving her time to question my desire for her, I retake her lips and move my hands to her hips.

"If you get naked, I won't be able to stop myself from taking you."

"And that's a problem?"

"It is if you want to leave this bathroom anytime soon."

"Leaving is overrated," she huffs.

"I'll come over tonight if you aren't too tired. Or we can wait until our date tomorrow," I suggest.

Another whine slips out. "I need you now. Show me you want me."

The hard dick in my pants is screaming at me to listen, but I will never forgive myself if our first time is in a club bathroom.

"Can't fuck you," I grit. "But I can make you come on my thigh. How does that sound, *Zlatíčko*? Think I can rub your hot pussy and get you off? I wonder if I can get you to moan loud enough that the assholes who've been eyeing you all night know you're taken."

She lets out a garbled "Yes!" as I use my grasp on her hips to move her up and down my thigh. I know no one will be able to hear her over the music but damn if I don't wish they could. It occurs to me that she never acknowledged what we are and I need to know we're on the same page.

"Tell me you're mine, and I'll make you come so hard you soak my jeans. Tell me you understand that this sweet body is mine and only mine, and I'll give you what you want."

"Yours," she mewls, chest heaving. "I'm yours."

"All mine. And I'm yours."

Her confirmation has me quickening my pace. When her hands grip my shoulder tighter, I know she's close.

"That's it, baby. Come for your man. Show me how hot it makes you to be mine." It only takes a few more seconds for her to let out a choked sob as her orgasm overtakes her.

My kisses turn soft as she comes down, and I release her hips. My thigh remains in place to hold her up as my hands rub down her sides. Her glassy gaze meets mine, and I can't help but smile at how gorgeous she is blissed out. I hate the thought that she has to go back out into a crowded club. I should demand she leave with me now, but I don't want to come off as a controlling asshole.

"Wow," she finally says. "I can't say I'm surprised that the best orgasm I've ever had is in a club bathroom, but I never thought it would be without someone else touching me. You put all my other bathroom escapades to shame."

I growl at the comment and nip at her lip, pinching her butt playfully. "Don't worry, *Zlatíčko*. It won't be that way for long. You haven't seen anything yet."

"Can I see more tonight?"

I nod. "I imagine the guys will want to spend the rest of the night here. I can follow you home after."

"I forgot they were here. You need to go back to them right now! They probably think we're in here fucking."

I give her an amused expression. Wasn't she begging me to do just that moments ago?

"They're fine," I assure her. "We'll go back out there when you're ready."

"Ready?" she questions before catching her reflection in the mirror over my shoulder and gasping. "I looked wrecked!"

A swell of pride erupts inside me. Her pink lipstick is smudged, her hair is disheveled, and her romper is out of whack.

"No need to be cocky about it," she grumbles.

"You'll see how cocky I am later."

She ushers me out of the bathroom. "Go back out there. I need to reapply my lipstick and fix this mess."

"You are beautiful." I nip at her jaw.

"You only think that because you made me this way. Now shoo, I'll come see you after I check on all my tables."

I kiss her until we're breathless one last time before leaving. My friends wisely say nothing when I rejoin them, and we spend the rest of the night enjoying ourselves while I watch my golden goddess float around the club.

TEN

Morgan

STANDING in the employee locker room, I rush to change out of my club outfit and into something comfier for the drive home. Thank God I dressed cute to come in tonight. I would be mortified to have Ralphie see me go from my sexy satin romper to baggy sweats, especially now that I know where this night is headed.

I don't know what happened to cause him to show up tonight, but I'm not disappointed in the outcome. My lips still tingle from his kisses hours later as my mind reels from his declaration. Don't get me started on the sensations pulsing through the rest of my body.

I am low key mortified by how wrecked I look from making out and humping his leg. I'm shocked he didn't change his mind. Instead, he seemed as if he wanted to devour me whole—something I hope happens later. Since I was parked in the employee lot, I told him to head to my place after last call. I'm only a few minutes behind him, but I plan to use the drive to psych myself up. It was easy to get lost in the moment, but now the nerves are setting in.

I would typically talk to Carina or maybe Madison, but it's too late to call either. Mads is out of town on a flight, and we aren't close enough for me to wake her up. Moments like this make me envious of people with close friend groups. Sure, I have tons of people I can call to party or attend a brand event, but not many who would be there for me in a pinch.

I used to lean on my brother for that, but now he's off playing ball in Texas. It's embarrassing that someone with fifteen thousand social media followers doesn't have someone she would consider a best friend, but here we are. Ugh, this is a depressing train of thought. It's not doing much to get me in the mood for the night that awaits me.

Grabbing my phone, I text Ralphie that I'm on my way and turn on my *Badass Bitch* playlist. It's the perfect combination of feminine rage and empowerment. A few songs in, I am interrupted by a response.

2:27 AM

RALPHIE

See you soon. I hope you sent this before you left and didn't text while driving.

ME

I would never

Don't worry. I can text through my speakers.

RALPHIE

That's good. You are too precious to risk. I need you intact for my plans for tonight.

Okay, swoon. How does he always say the sweetest and sexiest things? I don't think a single man I've dated has ever cared if I put myself at risk. They've also never kissed me with such possession that I could sense it in my bones.

Lost jamming to my playlist and replaying our bathroom encounter, I get home in record time. Pulling into the spot directly in front of my place, I smile when I see the large familiar frame walking toward me. Ralphie could have easily pulled into this spot. Instead, he left it free for me.

I open the car door before he reaches me. He takes me by surprise when he immediately crowds me and kisses the hell out of me.

"Hi," I greet when he pulls away.

"Hi."

"What was that?"

"A kiss?" he answers teasingly. "I assumed you were familiar with the concept after doing it earlier, but I am happy to demonstrate again. Inside."

Taken back by his playful side, I step in front of him to lead him into my apartment. Once there, I expect him to ravage me. After all, I felt how hard he was against my leg during our bathroom romp, and he didn't get any relief. But instead of dragging me straight to bed, he double-checks the locks and lumbers into the kitchen.

"Are you hungry?" he asks.

"What?"

"Are you hungry?" he says slower. "I don't know if you usually eat after work." He frowns as if not knowing that information upsets him.

"I usually drink cherry juice and wind down for bed by doing my skincare routine and listening to a few chapters of an audiobook."

He reaches out to pull a glass from the cabinet, but I place my hand over his to stop him. "That isn't my plan for tonight."

"No?" he questions, dropping his hand and turning toward me.

"Nuh uh. I'm not ready to sleep yet."

"What are you ready for?"

Instead of answering him, I palm his growing erection and lightly press my lips against his. He quickly deepens the kiss, hands sliding to my ass to pull me into him further. I can't play with him the way I want with our bodies this close. Instead, I settle for squeezing him over his jeans.

We're both panting when we break our kiss, and I want this man more than I've ever wanted anyone. The desire to please and keep him is overwhelming. "I didn't get to take care of you earlier," I whisper against his lips.

"Seeing you come apart for me was enough," he groans as I unbutton his jeans and slip my hand inside his boxers.

"Maybe for you." Stepping back from him, I drag his jeans and boxers down enough to free his dick as I kneel in front of him. I knew he was big from touching him, but Ralphie is packing. He isn't the longest man I've seen, but he's thick. So thick that I'm slightly worried about fitting him in my mouth.

"Morgan," he rasps as my hand circles his length. "You don't have to do that."

"I know." I say before licking the head. His salty flavor bursts onto my tongue. His hand drifts to cup my cheek when I swirl my tongue around his tip. He doesn't push me further but doesn't stop me either. He caresses me, peering down through hooded eyes.

Emboldened by his touch, I slowly suck him into my mouth. I can only get a few inches due to the girth, but you'd think I was deep-throating him based on the noises he makes. I've never gotten wet giving head before, but seeing him enjoy himself has me clenching my thighs together as I hollow my cheeks and suck harder.

I expect him to take over and thrust into my mouth, but he doesn't. He lets me lead. With one hand wrapped around his base and my tongue swirling around him, I suck in earnest. After a minute, he curses and pulls me off.

"No more. You're too good, and I am not blowing my load down your throat in your kitchen when your roommate could stumble in at any moment."

"She's out of town," I reply.

Eyes darkening, he pulls me up. "Which room is yours?"

"Second door on the right."

Next thing I know, Ralphie has me over his shoulder as he walks to my bedroom. Kicking the door shut behind him, he throws me down on the bed. Standing above me, he rips his shirt off over his head before leaning down to kiss me senseless.

"Back up on the bed. It's time for you to get naked, *Zlatíčko*," he commands.

His hands go to my leggings while mine drag off my shirt, leaving me in a lace bralette and thong.

"You are so sexy," he mutters.

"Back at ya. I want to see all of you."

"You first."

"Same time," I barter.

He must agree because he pushes his pants and boxers down in one swift movement as I unclasp the bra. He watches me, transfixed, as my thumbs hook into the waistband of my thong. Reveling in the attention, I pull it down slower than necessary. Staring at my center, Ralphie brings his eyes back to mine. The gleam in them is borderline feral as he puts one knee on the mattress and leans down to kiss my hip bones.

Hands trail down my thighs until he pushes them wider, opening me up to his scrutiny. I bite my lip as I watch him take me in. When he places a soft kiss directly on my clit, I shudder. His tongue gently traces my seam reverently until I'm squirming beneath him.

"Please," I beg when it becomes too much. I expect him to ignore me, but he heeds my cries instead. Bringing his thumbs to my center, he spreads me open and laps me with an urgency that makes me wonder which one of us has been teased most by his ministrations.

When he sucks my clit into his mouth, my hips buck up into his face. The moan he releases sends a shock through my system. His hands land back on my thighs, holding me in place.

"Please don't stop. I'm so close."

His grip pulses on my thighs, letting me know he hears me. He continues to suck and flick my bundle of nerves as he plunges one finger inside me. I'm so wet that he's met with no resistance when he adds a second, then a third. The stretch is exquisite. My cries grow louder as I clench around his fingers.

"Oh my God, yes." Warmth spreads through my lower belly as I crest higher and higher. As I'm about to reach my peak, he crooks his fingers, and I detonate. My chest lifts off the bed as he uses his free hand to hold down my pelvis and continue licking. I thrash against him.

"Fuck, fuck, sensitive," I pant.

With one more tender kiss to my clit, he pulls back, wiping evidence of my arousal on my thigh.

"One day, I'll keep licking you until you cover my face in your cum," he states, kissing up my body. He steals my breath in a filthy kiss before I can respond.

"I need you inside me, please."

"Condom?" I see panic in his expression. He must not have expected the night to end this way and didn't bring one.

"I have some, but I don't know if they're made for someone your size. I don't know if I was made for someone your size."

He laughs. "It'll fit. Both in the condom and in you. I'm not sure what some asshole told you, but regular condoms are plenty stretchy."

Moments later, he proves he does fit into the condom, which somewhat alleviates the nerves about him fitting inside me. Laying his body over mine, he kisses me softly as he positions himself between my legs. I squirm when he uses the head of his cock to tease my still-sensitive clit.

"Inside, please," I moan.

"You beg so sweetly; how can I say no?" In one thrust, he is seated completely. We both groan. Tension bleeds from his body as he allows me to adjust to him. When I wiggle against him, he nuzzles into my neck and slowly moves.

"So tight." Grabbing one leg, he slings it over my hip, allowing him to press deeper into me. "Damn it, babe. You can't clench on me if you want me to last."

"Who says I want you to last," I taunt. "You've already made me come twice tonight."

"It's not a competition. But I'm not letting go until you come on my cock. I'm going to find that spot that makes you see stars and draw every ounce of pleasure from this perfect body."

Swiveling his hips, he makes good on his word. The change in angle has him sliding against my walls, hitting every spot until my legs, both now wrapped around him, are shaking.

"There it is," he murmurs. Keeping his position, he speeds up his thrusts.

"Fuck, yes. Just like that. Don't stop."

"I won't stop. Not until you break for me. You're going to come on my cock and tip me over the edge. Aren't you, baby? You're going to be my good girl and use this hot little cunt to make me come?"

"Yes, yes, yes," I cry. I've been called a 'good girl' before, but the praise has never hit the way it does now. There isn't much I wouldn't do to please him at this point. I want this man on a visceral level. He must be able to tell.

"That's it. You were made to take me. Your pussy is fluttering so good against my cock. Come on, good girl. Shatter for me. Show me how much you love having me inside you."

That's all it takes to push me over the edge for the third time tonight. My nails dig into his arms as I clamp around him, riding out my orgasm as he jerks inside me. I melt into the pillows as Ralphie lands on his arms above me, careful not to put too much weight on me.

"I didn't spend enough time enjoying these tonight," he says as he kisses my sternum and nuzzles into my chest.

"Next time, big guy."

Lifting, he offers me a grin. It's pure and boyish. I know it's rare to see him this carefree. I want to bring this side of him out more often. Standing from the bed, he ventures into the bathroom, returning with a washcloth.

"I can do that." I motion to the cloth.

"So can I." He crawls back into bed behind me once he's satisfied I'm clean.

"Are we sleeping naked?"

"Mhmm, that way, if I want to play with you in the middle of the night, we don't have to get rid of your pesky clothes all over again."

"Makes sense," I yawn, pushing back into him.

"Goodnight, mine," is the last thing I hear before drifting off.

WHEN I WAKE UP, I'm still wrapped up in Ralphie. His arms are banded around my waist, keeping me tight against him, which I would usually love, but my bladder insists we have other plans. Carefully as I can, I extract myself. After doing my business, I get a glimpse of myself and gasp in shock.

Exhausted from the events of last night, I skipped out on my skin-care routine. Not only is my smeared makeup making its best raccoon impression, but my hair is giving caught-in-wind-tunnel vibes. Peeking into my room, I see Ralphie still fast asleep, now hugging my pillow. I want to snap a picture of the adorable sight, but if I want to appear presentable, time is of the essence.

I quickly wash my face and slap on a glow serum and moisturizer. After brushing out my waves, I sprinkle dry shampoo into my hair to add back volume and counteract the oiliness from having his hands in it all night. With a quick curl of my lashes and coat of mascara, I finish with an application of cream blush and tinted ChapStick. It's nowhere near the glam I usually rock, but it's enough to stop him from running for the hills.

Tiptoeing back into the room, I slide back into bed. I must have jostled him because moments later, he stirs. Realizing he's holding a pillow, he flips on his back and pulls me toward him, slinging my leg over his.

"Morning, baby," he murmurs in a graveling morning voice that should be illegal. His accent is strongest when he is sleepy.

"Good morning," I reply. He smiles at my words and finally opens his eyes. I watch as he scans my face, brow furrowing.

"Everything okay?" I ask self-consciously. I thought I did enough to freshen up this morning, but apparently not.

"You look perfect," he says. But it doesn't sound like a compliment.

"Thank you?"

"No, I mean you're always perfect," he corrects, weighing his words. "You just don't look as if you had three mind-blowing orgasms last night. I guess I expected you to be more rumpled. I should have known you'd wake up angelic."

I blush at his response. "I washed my face and fluffed my hair when I used the bathroom."

Shaking the disappointed expression off his face, he kisses my forehead. "I know we didn't have plans until later, but do you want to grab brunch instead?"

"I'd love that. Let me get ready, and then we can head out."

"All you need to do is change clothes," he notes.

I laugh at the suggestion until I realize he is serious. "I could never go out without a full face, especially with you. I need to shower and redo my hair. I won't take long, I promise."

"You can take as long as you need, *Zlatíčko*. But know, you never need to do anything to be seen with or by me. I adore you exactly the way you are."

I blink at him, no idea how to respond. Instead of waiting for me to, he scoops me up in his arms.

"Now that you mention it, I think you definitely need a shower. Let's do that together. I bet I can dirty you up again before I scrub you clean." And he does.

We stay in the shower until the water grows cold, then reluctantly head out to brunch at the kolache cafe. Early in the afternoon, Ralphie has to return home to do the things he would have done this morning, but we agree to grab lunch tomorrow before I set off on my next flight.

I don't want to get my hopes up, but this feels like the start of something incredible. I can only hope my intuition is right.

ELEVEN

Ralphie

THE PAST FEW weeks with Morgan have been incredible. We mostly stayed in our bubble, avoiding the press and anywhere gawkers might pop up. I'm not hiding our relationship, but I don't want Morgan to have to deal with the scrutiny that comes with dating an NHL player until it's absolutely necessary.

I get the idea that she is usually out at more parties and influencer events than she has been this month, but since one of her coworkers had to take unexpected leave to care for a sick parent, she's been flying more. I wouldn't mind if I weren't going into training camp.

My next three weeks will be filled with games, team meetings, and strategy sessions. The only silver lining is that we'll be in town. If our schedules line up, I might be able to meet her for lunch or coffee. I won't hold my breath, though. At least we can still text and call.

"You're later than usual," Danvers notes as I enter the locker room for our first practice. I'm used to his out-of-pocket comments by now. I simply ignore him, which he hates only slightly less than my pretending to appease his concerns. I spent last night with Morgan and very reluctantly left her in my bed to make it here. It may not be my typical hour early, but there is still a solid twenty minutes before we hit the ice.

"D, it's not your business when people get here as long as they're on time," Mikelson chides.

"Why not?"

"Because it just isn't," our big man sighs.

"Keeping the kid in line is aging you," Connor teases him.

"Someone has to do it," Mikelson replies. "And I don't see you volunteering."

"I manage the grump. Besides, Danvers catching social cues would be as shocking as Nokavik getting a movie reference. Let the kid sink or swim on his own. If he's ballsy enough to poke the bear, then he is ballsy enough to get his ass mauled."

"In case it wasn't clear, you're the bear," he directs my way.

"Got that," I respond.

Sitting in the chair beside my locker, Connor continues to engage me in conversation as I get into my gear. "Haven't seen you around as much."

"Been busy."

"Busy with a blonde smokeshow?"

"Maybe. What's it to you?" I narrow my eyes at him.

"It's rude for me to ask why he's late but not for Connor to ask about his girlfriend?" Danvers asks. I don't hear Mikelson's answer as I refocus my attention on my friend.

"Touchy, touchy," Connor laughs. "I'm happy for you. I wouldn't have picked you to be the next man down, but I think it's great."

"If you're that lonely and missing me, I bet Morgan has a friend she can introduce you to," I tease.

"If all you fuckers keep falling in love on me, I might take you up on that." Patting my shoulder, he gets up to greet players who arrived while I sit there with my world completely rocked.

Love? Do I *love* Morgan? It is way too soon to admit that, but I don't hate the idea of it. I don't know if I'm ready to say I love her, but I am getting there. Despite her bubbly energy opposing my chill demeanor, she is a balm to my soul. She's a lighthouse in a storm, calling out to me and showing me the way home. If things keep going the way they are, it won't take long for me to be ready to say those three little words.

It's time I told Andre about what's happening. I've held off because I didn't want to hear all his ideas on how I can use this relationship to my advantage. But at this point, people will spot us out sooner rather than later, and I'd prefer we have a game plan in place for protecting my girl.

THIS YEAR'S camp was more grueling than any I've participated in. Maybe it's because the rookies were not up to par. Or maybe for the first time since I was drafted, I had somewhere else I wanted to be. Morgan and I were only able to meet up twice in the last three weeks and both were quick. To say I miss her is an understatement.

We were supposed to grab lunch yesterday, but she canceled on me at the last minute. She also hasn't texted me all day, which is unlike her. It may be overstepping, but I am headed to her place to see what's up. The guys would tell me I am being too intense, but I can't shake the feeling that something is wrong.

When I pull up to her place, I notice her car out front. That's good; it means she's home. After a few knocks, the door swings open, and Madison answers.

We both stand there staring at one another until I break the silence. "Is Morgan home?"

"Does she know you're coming?"

"I texted her."

"That's not really the same thing."

"Can I come in? I want to check and make sure she's okay. She is okay, right?"

"If you consider puking her guts out for eighteen hours, okay, then sure. It's perfect you're here, actually. I was about to go to my boyfriend's for unobstructed bathroom access."

My gut swells with worry and fury. Her roommate is sick, and

Madison was going to leave her here on her own. What if she needed something or got worse?

As Madison heads toward her room, I barrel into the apartment. The bathroom is empty, meaning Morgan must be in her room. I knock softly on the door but open it without waiting for a response. My girl is curled up in a ball on her side, covers thrown fitfully off.

Approaching the bed, I push sweaty blonde strands off her face. Pressing my lips to her forehead, I can tell she has a slight temperature. I want to give her something for it, but I don't know if she's taken anything already. Her useless roommate is already gone, though I doubt she would have known. I have no choice but to wake Morgan up.

"Baby," I coo. "Baby, can you wake up for me?"

Her eyes blink open slowly. "Ralphie? Wh-what are you doing here?"

"I came to check on you when you didn't answer me all day. I'm glad I did. You need someone to take care of you."

"What? No. You can't be here. I'm sick. You'll get sick. I got a stomach bug from a passenger on yesterday's flight. You can't get sick before the first game of the season."

"I have a few days before then. I'll be fine. Plus, I have an iron stomach."

"You shouldn't see me like this," she whines. The sound hurts my heart.

Despite our conversation that first morning, seeing Morgan looking anything but perfect is a rarity. Even on nights we plan only to watch a movie, she comes over made up. She finally stopped putting on makeup in the mornings after nights she did her skincare routine. She may have thought I didn't know, but I pay too close attention to her not to notice when her blonde eyelashes are black.

"I should absolutely see you like this. I don't want you only at your best, *Zlatíčko*. I want your worst, too. Let me take care of you."

Before she can argue, another wave of cramps passes through her, and she clutches her stomach in pain.

"Have you taken anything?" I ask.

"Can't. Keep It. Down," she pants. The pitiful whimpers that leave her lips are almost my undoing.

"Hold tight. I'm going to fix it."

Pulling my phone out of my pocket, I dial the one number I think can help.

"This better be good," Fitz grumbles. "I haven't had any time with my woman during camp."

"It's your 'woman' I want to talk to," I say, skipping the pleasantries.

"Why?"

"Can you put Tabby on the phone? Please." I add that last part to remind myself not to snap at my friend and that I need the expertise of his nurse wife.

"I'll put it on speaker," he begrudgingly agrees.

"What's up, Nokavik?" a feminine voice asks through the phone.

"How do you treat the stomach bug?"

"Yikes. That's been going around. Are you sure you have it? I think you'd be puking your guts up by now."

"I don't have it. Someone else does."

"Oh. OH! Is this the girlfriend Fitzy has been telling me about?"

"Yeah," I say before she can waste time with any more questions. "She has a slight fever and hasn't been able to keep anything down. What can I do?"

"How long has she been sick?"

"Eighteen hours, give or take."

"Geez, okay. She is past the worst of it now, I'd imagine. She needs fluids with electrolytes. Ginger tea and chicken broth can also help. Don't give her anything but water until an hour after vomiting, if you can. She'll be more likely to keep it down.

"As far as her fever goes, if it isn't too high, she should sweat it out. It's a sign her body is fighting the illness, but a room-temperature bath or shower will cool her off in a pinch. If not, acetaminophen is your best bet. You can also use a wet washcloth to help cool her off.

"She'll need plenty of rest, and you should disinfect anything she touches to keep it from spreading. If you've already had contact with her, it may be too late for you."

"I'll be fine. Thank you for the advice."

"Let me know if you need anything else."

"Thank you. I'll let Fitz have you back now."

"Thank Christ," I hear muttered through the phone, followed by a yelp of pain.

Ending the call, I pull up my grocery delivery app and order everything I need. She may already have some of it, but better safe than sorry. I include chicken soup from a deli I know she loves. I will have been here for over an hour by the time it gets here. If she doesn't get sick again, I can get fluids in her right away.

I desperately want to give her something to regulate her fever, but I don't want to stop her body from doing its job. Running a washcloth under the water, I head back into her bedroom to wait for provisions to arrive.

TWELVE

Morgan

GROANING, I turn over in my bed, exhausted but less sticky than expected. My fever must have finally broken. I am surprisingly clean and… wearing different pajamas. I don't remember changing, but I'm glad not to wake up a sweaty mess. I must have had more of a fever than I thought because I had some wild dreams. Dreams where rough hands soothed me, and kind eyes took care of me—crazy stuff.

Slapping around my bedside table, I don't find my phone. I must have left it in my bag. As much as I want to stay wrapped up in bed, I have no clue what time it is or if anyone has been attempting to contact me. Willing myself to move, I get up and enter the living room. As I do, the door to my apartment opens, causing me to let out a yelp and grab the nearest object to defend myself.

"What are you doing up?" a concerned, familiar voice asks.

"You scared me!" I shout at Ralphie. My initial shock bleeds into confusion as I clutch my chest. "What are you doing here? How did you get in?"

"I took the key from your purse when I went to grab coffee. The

"

selection you have is abysmal. It's all flavored garbage. Once your fever broke, I figured it was safe to leave you alone for a minute."

"Hey! My coffee selection is fantastic. We can't all survive on bitter bean juice the way you do. You didn't answer my question. How did you get inside in the first place?"

"Madison let me in."

"She did? Where is she?"

"She left after I got here last night."

"Last night?!" I squeak.

"Yes. Who do you think has been taking care of you?"

I attempt to cover my eyes with my hands but end up hitting myself in the face with the picture frame I'm holding.

"That wasn't a dream?"

"It was not," he replies as his lips twitch. "Why are you holding that?"

"I thought there was an intruder!"

"And you were going to fend me off with a picture of you and your brother sitting on what I hope is a consenting Santa's lap?" He's broken out into a full grin now.

"What? Oh, that. Rob and I gifted my mom with recreated pictures of us from childhood for Mother's Day a few years ago. I loved this one since I've never seen a Santa so flustered. I had to have a copy."

"I don't blame him. But back to my original question: why are you up? You should be resting. You were more out of it than I realized if you thought my presence was a dream."

I flush as I process the knowledge that every sweet word and kind touch was Ralphie. I hate to admit it didn't seem plausible. "It felt real at the moment, but reflecting on it this morning, it sounded far-fetched."

"What did?"

"That you would be here taking care of me. I mean, why would you do that when I was vomiting everywhere? Oh my God! Did you see me throw up?" This time, I put the frame down before burying my face in my hands.

"None of that," he tsks, walking over from the entry and pulling my hands away. "You have nothing to be embarrassed about. The puking portion of the evening passed before I got here, but I wouldn't have minded if you did. I don't think you understand how gross a hockey locker room can be. Bodily fluids are everywhere."

I know he means blood and guts, but the mental image in my head goes a different way. He must be able to read my mind because his eyes darken.

"None of that either. I don't want to spank you while you're sick, but I will if you don't drop whatever image you conjured up in there," he says, tapping my temple.

I roll my eyes but lean into his touch when he leaves his hand on my head. "You didn't have to come take care of me. I'm sorry if Madison called you."

"She didn't call me. You should have, though."

"She didn't? Then how did you know? And why on earth would I have called you?"

"I knew because after you canceled and I didn't hear from you, I got worried and dropped by. And you should have called me because I'm your man, and you needed someone to take care of you."

"You would have wanted to be here while I puked my guts out?" I ask in disbelief.

"Yes," he replies instantly.

"Why?"

"Because you're mine, *Zlatičko*. It's my job to make sure you're okay."

With no idea how to respond to the conviction in his statement, I change the subject. "I probably shouldn't have coffee after being sick."

"I agree. That's why I got you tea and oatmeal. I know you prefer berries, but bananas are better for an upset stomach." Walking past me into the kitchen, he sets down our drinks and a white paper sack.

"You didn't have to do all that. I could've made toast."

He pins me with a glare but otherwise ignores my statement. "You ready to eat? You also need to drink some water with electrolytes."

"Let me brush my teeth first. My mouth tastes how a trash can smells."

Entering the bathroom, I gasp at my appearance. My typically tame hair is a wavy mess as if I went to bed with it wet, which I never do.

My face is surprisingly makeup-free but also pale and missing my usual glow. I guess I skipped my skincare routine, too.

After brushing my teeth and washing my face, I grab the next product in my morning regime when Ralphie's voice cuts through the door. "I hope you aren't dolling yourself up in there. Your food is getting cold, and you're beautiful as you are."

I open the door to face him. "If you think this is beautiful, we need to seriously raise your expectations. I look horrendous. Did all the sweat go to my hair? I don't understand why my body is clean, but my hair resembles Mia Thermopolis' before her makeover."

"I don't get that reference, but your body is clean because I showered you last night. It was the best way to lower your fever without medicating you. I washed your hair, too, but I wasn't sure which of those million products you used on it after the shower." Pink crawls up his neck, and his expression is almost sheepish. I'd admire how cute it was if I weren't stunned.

"You washed my hair?"

"Yes." He nods. "I'm sorry if you didn't want me to. But your hair *was* sweaty, and a lot of temperature regulation goes through your head, so—oof."

I fling myself into his chest, wrapping my arms around his middle. As I sniff back tears, he cups my face and tips my head up to search my face.

"I can't remember the last time someone took care of me that way. Sure, I've showered with men before, but getting me clean was the last thing on their minds."

When his nostrils flare, I giggle.

"You deserve to be taken care of, *Zlatičko*. But maybe don't mention showering with other men again, yeah?"

"I can do that," I murmur, nose back in his sternum.

"Come on. I need to feed you, and then we can curl up on the couch and watch those annoying housewomen."

THIRTEEN

Morgan

I SHIFT NERVOUSLY as the usher checks my ticket outside the suite area of National Bank Arena. When Ralphie asked me to go to his game, I assumed it would be in the stands. Nope, he got me a ticket for the family suite. If I would have known, I wouldn't have dressed for the chill of the ice.

After handing me back my phone, the employee walks me down the hall and into the room. As I enter, the weight of several pairs of eyes land on me. I immediately shrink, taking my suitemates in. They may not be dressed to the nines, but they are more dressed up than me. There isn't a team logo in sight. I offer them a tight smile as I smooth down my dad's '90s-era jersey that I paired with my recently finished beanie and leggings.

The women around me quickly refocus their attention back to their conversations, and I let out a sigh of relief. Heading to the front of the suite, I survey the scene in front of me. From this high, we have a perfect view of the entire arena. Mesmerized by the players skating around for warm-ups, I don't notice someone saddle up beside me. When she clears her throat, I startle.

"Apologies," she says smoothly. "I didn't mean to scare you. I wanted to introduce myself. I'm Veronica. My husband is the team captain, which makes me like the de facto captain of the WAGs."

"Hi," I reply, taking her hand. "WAGs?"

"Industry lingo," she responds with a flip of her hair. "Wives and girlfriends. It takes a lot to support our men off the ice. We get together to ensure their needs and obligations are met."

"Makes sense. And I'm Morgan, Ralp-Nokavik's girlfriend."

I'm then struck by the fact that I don't know what people call him. I've heard his teammates call him a few different things, but I haven't interacted with them outside the clubs.

"It's nice to meet you. I didn't realize he was seeing anyone."

"It's new. Not new-new, but new for this season," I stammer.

"Well, welcome. I love your hat."

"Thank you." My fingers instinctively rise to touch the project I worked on during my downtime traveling last week. It has teal and light blue stripes, the Crush's colors, and faux fur pompom on top. On the front, I added Ralphie's number since I wasn't sure if he wanted me to get a jersey with his name on it. The books I've read have made that seem like a big gesture.

"Enjoy the game, Morgan. I'm sure I'll see you around," she states as another woman beckons for her. Everything about her was perfectly lovely, but I can't help thinking she wasn't sincere. I chalk it up to my own insecurities. Making a small plate from the buffet and grabbing a drink, I settle into a seat as the pregame announcements begin.

At the end of the first period, the seltzers I drank sit heavy in my bladder. I didn't intend to drink more than one, but seeing Ralphie charging through giant men swiping at him with sticks left me unsettled. Not wanting to miss any action, I use intermission to stretch my legs and take care of business.

The bathroom on the suite level is nicer than on the others I've been to. This may be my first hockey game, but I've attended NBA games here before. I need to find out how they switch between wood and ice because you can't tell another sport shares this facility.

As I am about to flush the toilet, a group of women enter the space. "Can you believe how casually she came to the game? You'd think she would want to impress us or, at the very least, her man."

"You would think," another says. "I looked her up on social media, and based on her pictures, we should be glad she came in as much clothing as she did. She is usually decked out in short skirts and sparkles. All her posts scream, 'Look at me! Look at me!' There is nothing less cute than attention-seeking behavior."

"Shut up. Let me see! How did you get her name?"

"Since the family room falls under my domain, I always know the suite attendees. Radek had to tell John her name to get her on the list. I knew who she was the moment she walked in."

"What else did he say about her?"

"Not much," she huffs. "You know men, they hardly ask follow-up questions. From what I can tell, she's local, a flight attendant, and works as a bottle girl/influencer on the side."

Great, three of them are talking shit about me in a semi-public place, and I either have to confront them or wait them out in this stall.

"A bottle girl?" a third woman snorts. "I wouldn't have thought that was Nokavik's type. I've seen the bunnies who throw themselves at him. To be honest, she looks like one in those photos. I figured he would go for someone with a little more class."

"I heard they met her at Fitz's bachelor party, so who knows if that's *all* she is. Nothing would surprise me based on the amount of cleavage she's showing in those pictures."

"Please," mean girl number two scoffs. "Fitz wouldn't dream of cheating on Tabby. He's smitten."

"You never know," Veronica notes. "These men get propositioned every day. It's only a matter of time until they give in. You simply have to ensure what he has waiting for him at home beats what he gets on the road."

"And that he gives you pretty things to ease his guilt," number three singsongs. "How do you think Kelly got that new Benz? What happens in Vegas sometimes ends up in your wife's DMs."

"We'll see how long Morgan lasts. Everything about her screams flighty airhead. She'll either annoy him until he breaks up with her, or she'll get bored and move on to a D-list actor. A girl like that is always searching for the next stepping stone. She would never be able to handle this lifestyle."

"Where did she run off to anyway?"

"Who knows? I'm simply happy for the break from looking at that truly awful beanie."

The sound of their laughter trails out of the bathroom. I'm used to mean girls, but I didn't expect to face them right out of the gate. I steel myself to return to the suite as I wash my hands. Before I can leave, though, someone else exits a stall.

The tiny brunette's expression resembles mine as we make eye contact in the mirror. She's dressed as casually as I am in leggings and a vest.

"You heard all that too, huh?" she questions.

"I'm afraid I was the star of that conversation."

"Morgan?!"

My tight smile must give her the answer she hoped for since she practically bowls me over with her hug. "I'm Tabby. It's nice to meet you finally. I've heard all about you!"

"You mean aside from that?"

She wrinkles her nose. "Yes, aside from that. Don't let them get to you. Stacy and Becka have been with their players for years without them making things legal, and Veronica's husband has a girlfriend in practically every city. They're bitter WAGs and jealous you landed the golden goose."

"Ralphie is the golden goose?"

"You call him 'Ralphie?' Omigod, that's adorable! And yes, he is. That man is so loyal he won't even use a different brand of stick tape. There is no way he would cheat on his partner. He is one of the high-est-paid players on the team, and he has years left in his career. They undoubtedly wanted to set one of their snooty friends up with him. Unfortunately for them, he fell for you!"

"I don't know about that," I reply, thinking about everything the catty WAGs said. Am I the right type of woman for him? I can only imagine the options he has available. It's hard to believe he'd settle for someone who barely graduated high school and spends her weekends faking nice to the rich and famous for tips.

"We'll see," Tabby chirps. "Come on. We can sit together. I rushed here after my shift and am famished. I hope they have a good spread today."

When we walk back into the suite, the gazes of Veronica and her cronies burn into my skin. As much as I try not to let their words get to me, I spend the rest of the game wondering if I have what it takes to be the partner Ralphie needs.

FOURTEEN

Ralphie

ADRENALINE IS RUSHING through me after our win against Calgary. The first game of the season sets the tone for the rest of the year. If tonight is any indication, we are going to kick ass. I ride that high all the way to the parking lot. I told Morgan to meet me at my place after the game. She could have waited in the tunnel, but I didn't want to overwhelm her. It can get wild down there, especially after a win.

"Nokavik, wait!" someone calls from behind me. Seconds later, Fitz and Tabby catch up to me.

"I didn't know you'd be here tonight, Tabby. Did you sit in the suite?"

"I did. Morgan is an absolute peach," she gushes. I smile at her assessment of my girl.

"I couldn't agree more. Did she have fun?" Something in Tabby's expression gives me pause.

"She mostly had a nice time," she hesitates. "She didn't love seeing you get smashed around, but I think she enjoyed watching you do the smashing."

"That all?"

"There may have been an incident with Veronica and some of the other WAGs."

Veronica is the wife of our team captain. She takes charge of the family suite and other shit like team dinners and the holiday party. She has been nice enough to me, but I've heard some guys grumbling about her being rude to their girlfriends.

"What happened?"

Tabby lips thin into an apologetic grimace. "I got here during the first intermission and when I went to the bathroom, a few women were there saying less than flattering things about Morgan. When I came out of my stall, she was there. The expression on her face told me she overheard them, too.

"I told her not to listen to them, and we had fun for the rest of the game, but I think it affected her more than she let on. I doubt she'll mention it to you, but I thought you should know before seeing her later in case she seems off."

"Thank you for telling me, Tabs."

"Of course. I like her. I think she's good for you."

"She is," I reply with a tight smile. "See you later."

Driving to my place, I wonder what they could have been saying about my perfect girl. Her self-esteem is already fragile from dating Chet, the douche canoe, and whoever else came before him. I've been working hard to lift her, but every time she thanks me for basic decency, it makes me want to choke him out all over again.

WHEN I GET to my place, Morgan is waiting in her car, scrolling through her phone, oblivious to my approach. Upon closer inspection, she is scrolling through her own social media profile. I think she is looking for something specific, but the further she goes, the deeper her frown.

When I tap on her window, she jumps and clutches her chest.

Opening her door, I guide her to the front of my house. It's not a mansion like some of my teammates have, but it's a decent size, especially for LA. I wasn't as concerned about the size as the location. It's in a prime spot near the stadium, but it's secluded enough that I never see any neighbors, which is precisely how I want it.

Morgan is tense as she puts her bag on the entry bench and walks into the kitchen. Opening the fridge, she surveys its contents before shutting it without grabbing anything.

"Hungry?" I ask. Her shoulders shrug in response. "Thirsty?"

"Meh."

"Do you want to tell me what's bothering you?"

Her eyes snap to mine at the question. They are pooled with apprehension, which I hate. Moving toward her, I cage her against the refrigerator doors, hands on either side of her head.

"Tell me, *Zlatičko*. I can't fix it if I don't know what it is."

She blows out a raspberry. "You don't have to fix everything in my life. Don't worry about it. I'm just in a mood."

"Of course, I have to fix everything in your life, especially your moods. Your happiness matters to me. Did something happen at the game? You had fun with Tabby, yeah?"

"Tabby was great." Her lips tip momentarily before a sad expression covers her pretty face. "It was fine. I enjoyed watching you play, though I didn't appreciate that one guy who kept slamming you into the boards. What was his problem?"

"It's his job, baby," I laugh. "Don't worry. I gave as good as I got. But I still can't shake the feeling that something is wrong with you."

Pulling her lip between her teeth, she averts her gaze, pondering her next words. "Are you ever worried I'm not cut out for this?"

"Cut out for what?"

"To be your girlfriend."

"Why would you ask that?" I question, rearing back.

"I don't know. My schedule is as crazy as yours. And you are a private guy. You stay away from the limelight as much as possible, whereas I thrive on attention. I enjoy going to places where I'll be seen, wearing loud clothing, and going full glam for everyday errands. That's not you. It makes me wonder if we're suited for each other."

"Suited," I repeat.

"Yes, suited." Morgan squares her shoulders as she stares into my eyes. She may be putting on a brave face, but I see the fragility behind her mask. I want—no, need—her to know she doesn't have to have that with me, and she sure as shit doesn't have to act or be a certain way.

"Don't you think you'd be happier long term with someone less loud, less extra, just… less." Her voice fades into a whisper.

Stepping fully into her space, I silence her. "I'm going to stop you right there. There is no one I could be happier with than you. I love that you enjoy dressing up and having all eyes on you. Anyone who isn't looking at you has to be blind because you steal focus in every room you enter.

"And in regards to someone else being more 'suited' for me, that's a load of shit. You are perfect for me because you are you. I don't want quiet or demure or *less*. If anything, I want more. I will never get enough of you. Your light calls to me and beckons me home. You are mine. And I want you exactly as you are."

"Are you sure?"

"I've never been more sure of anything in my life. Let me prove it to you." Without preamble, I reach down to her thighs and pull her up my body. She instinctively wraps her legs around my waist as I walk us into the living room. Once there, I settle on the couch with her straddling my hips. Reminiscent of our first hookup at Clamatis, I grind her up and down my lap.

"You are stunning. Every inch. I am going to spend all night worshiping you to prove exactly how perfect you are."

She mewls into my mouth, and I swallow the sound. Her hands grasp my shoulder as she rocks against me, but it isn't enough. She needs more, and I need to give her more.

I can't help the twitch of my lips at the sound of protest she makes when I pause our movements. Placing her on her feet in front of me, I slide off the couch. She stares at me, puzzled. Her confusion momentarily abates as I pull her leggings and panties down in one go.

"Put your knees on the couch and grab the back," I say. She moves to step beside me, but I stop her. "No, right here."

"But then I'll be kneeling over you."

"That's the idea, *Zlatíčko*. I want this pretty pussy hovering over my face so I can worship it the way it deserves."

"Ralphie," she hesitates. Her argument halts on her lips as I grip her thighs and pull her straight into my waiting mouth. Her knees hit the edge of the couch as my lips make contact with her center.

"Lean forward," I command.

She shivers as my breath ghosts across her, sensitive from grinding on my cock. When she obeys, I reward her by lazily licking at her clit. It only takes a few swipes for her to grip the couch tighter as her knees press harder into the cushion.

Using my hands to hold her ass, I spread her wider, gaining more access. She pushes against my touch, deliciously asking for more. Sliding down further, I thrust my tongue into her as one of my thumbs presses into her bundle of nerves.

Something switches in my brain as her legs shake around me, and I turn feral. I lick and suck and nip until she's thrashing above me.

"Baby," she cries, pulling against my hold while at the same time pushing into me harder. Overwhelmed with pleasure, she doesn't know if it's too much or not enough.

Maintaining my grip, one hand travels down to my aching cock. I clumsily pull it out of my pants and slowly stroke it to alleviate some of the mounting pressure. Having her this close to coming undone for me has me desperate to do the same. But I won't, not yet. I told her I was going to show her how much I wanted her, and I meant it.

Pulling back from her soaked core, I peer up into her eyes. "You drive me crazy. I need you to come for me, Morgan. I need you to come grinding down on my face."

"I want to come on your cock," she whines.

"You will. Show me how prettily you can come on my face, and then I'll fill this sweet pussy up with my cock. Can you do that for me?" When she doesn't respond, I nip at her inner thigh. "Can you be a good girl and come on my face?"

Her shaky nod is the affirmation I need to dive back in. When I suck her clit, she bucks wildly, and I know she is close. Not relenting in my pressure, I flick my tongue across her until she shudders through her release.

Scooting out from under her, I leave her knees on the couch. Keyed up from the sensation of her coming on my face, I quickly shuck off my clothing, marveling at her in my team colors. Only when I spot the name on the back do I notice the material's age.

Morgan has on a vintage sweater. I assumed she was wearing my name or a blank jersey. Seeing another name on her back has me growling. "Off!"

"What?" She turns her head to study me behind her, eyes still hazy from orgasm.

Stepping behind her, I wrap my arm around her waist and pull her up. Without explanation, I grab the hem of the jersey and yank it over her head.

"I thought you would enjoy seeing me in your colors."

"I did. I do. But no chance in hell are you coming on my cock with some other fucker's name on your back."

"Peterson has been retired for fifteen years." Amusement washes across her features.

I wrap my hand around her hair and hold her against my chest. The heat of her body against mine ratcheting my need higher. My cock nestles against her lips, coating itself with her earlier release. This new angle allows me to whisper directly in her ear. "I don't care if he's been retired for one hundred and fifty years. When I'm inside you, the only name you'll wear, think, scream, remember is mine."

With that declaration, I slam inside her. We both groan at the sudden intrusion. Giving her a moment to adjust, I rip the bra she was still wearing off and palm her breasts. When she squirms against me, I know she's ready for me to move.

One hand on her breast and the other on her hip, I slowly slide out and back in. She grips the arm that holds her to me, nails digging into my skin. The sensation makes me that much wilder, and I thrust more forcefully.

Wanting to give her all of me, I release my hold on her chest and press her toward the back of the couch, where she lays her elbows. The new angle allows her to take me deeper, and I watch in fascination as my cock disappears inside her. Her moans grow louder as I hit that spot inside her that makes me see stars.

"Fuck, I will never get over how perfect your pussy is. So tight and warm wrapped around me." She is velvet enveloping me, and I fight every second to maintain my composure.

Morgan babbles incoherently as I slam inside her over and over. Her walls contract around me as she nears her climax. Needing her to get there before I explode, I curl a hand between her legs to toy with her clit.

"Come for me, baby. Grip me like a vise." Her pussy tightens minutely, and I grit my teeth, thinking about anything I can to stave off my release. Roasted cabbage, the old men swimming at the YMCA, Danvers explaining to me for the fifteenth time the 'right' battleship strategy, none of it is helping. Doubling my efforts, I rub faster.

"You're taking me so well. Be a good girl, and come on my cock, Morgan." Seconds later, she does and it is my name on her lips.

FIFTEEN

Morgan

"YOU'RE NOT UP YET, *KAMARÁD*?" a male voice yells, waking me from a perfect night's sleep. After the couch, Ralphie brought me back to his bed and took his time worshipping every inch of my body. I expected to wake up wrapped in his arms, which I am. But I didn't expect to hear someone shouting outside his bedroom door.

"Ralphie," I whisper. When he doesn't stir, I nudge him. "Ralphie!"

"What?" he groans, groggily.

"Someone is inside your house." That statement jolts him awake.

"What?"

"A man is calling for you outside the room."

"Stay here," he commands. Springing into action, Ralphie yanks on a pair of boxes and grabs a spare hockey stick—a much better weapon against an intruder than a picture frame. Since my clothes and bag are in the central area of the house, I dress in one of his shirts. If this is an intruder, I don't want to run through this ritzy neighborhood nude. The quiet murmuring of voices instead of shouts leads me to believe we are not about to be burgled or ax-murdered.

91

Minutes later, Ralphie returns. "It's my agent. He made an impromptu visit since I ignored his postgame call."

"Why did you do that?"

Prowling toward me, he leans over where I am sitting on the bed and fuses our mouths in a savage kiss.

"I had more pressing matters to attend to. Come out and meet him."

"Okay," I pant, still breathless. Ralphie wears a self-satisfied smirk when he sees what I'm wearing.

"My clothes are out there. Oh my God! My clothes are out there. He can see my underwear!"

Hooking me around the waist, he stops my mad scramble and pushes me against the door. "First, you can wear my clothes whenever you want. In fact, I prefer seeing you in things that mark you as mine. Second, I put your clothes from last night in your overnight bag, which is now in the bathroom, if you want to clean up first."

"Thank you."

"I've always got you, *Zlatíčko*. Join us when you're ready. I'm going to order breakfast from the cafe."

ONE QUICK BUT vigorous shower and shortened morning routine later, I make my way into the kitchen right as Ralphie is plating the food.

"Ah, there is the woman I have been learning all about this morning," the man across from him calls. Ralphie's agent, Andre Svoboda, is in his mid-forties if his salt and pepper hair is anything to go on. From what I can tell, he isn't in hockey player shape but is decently fit. He has thick brows and features similar enough to Ralphie that I can see the shared heritage, but not so much that they appear related.

"Hello," I greet with a small wave. Ralphie motions for me to come to him, and I tuck into his side. I am usually a social butterfly. Meeting new people is my thing. But something about Andre leaves me with an uneasy sensation in my gut.

"Radek was telling me how the two of you connected. I was

surprised he didn't mention it sooner, but the man loves to keep me on my toes."

Ralphie grunts in response.

"Tell me about yourself, Morgan. I'm sure you know Radek isn't a big talker."

I think he talks the perfect amount to balance my chatterbox nature, but I keep that assessment to myself. Swallowing a bite of a delicious raspberry kolache, I ponder what he might want to know.

"Let's see, I'm twenty-four, born and raised in Long Beach, and have been a flight attendant for the last few years."

"And you also work at a nightclub?" he prods. I can't tell if there is any judgment in his tone, but I nod.

"Two, but they are owned by the same company. When I have free nights. It hardly feels like work to help people have fun."

"Ah, more of a hobby than a profession, then?"

"I wouldn't say that. It makes up a good amount of my income. You'd be surprised how much people are willing to pay to feel important."

"I can only imagine. It is nice when your hobbies can be profitable. Money is what talks in this town. I've seen time and time again how it can change people or be used in unscrupulous ways. Are you a big hockey fan?"

I get it now. He thinks I'm after Ralphie for his money. He's sizing me up. That's fine. It's his job to protect his client.

"Crocheting is my biggest hobby. I also enjoy cooking. And last night was my first hockey game. I am more of a baseball girl."

"Morgan's brother was drafted by Seattle earlier this year," Ralphie interjects.

"How nice," the other man responds. "Well, I don't want to take up too much of your time. I will be on my way if you could grab those contracts."

Ralphie nods and heads into his office. When he leaves, Andre's scrutinizing gaze shifts back to me.

"I don't know what game you're playing with the fake sunshine act, girly, but I am on to you. I've seen your type before and won't let you derail the career we've built."

"We?" This guy has a lot of nerve and I have not had enough coffee to reign in the sass.

"You know what I mean. Get the idea that he will fund your life-style out of that pretty little head now. Men like Radek can only have one focus, and his is hockey. You have him mesmerized right now with your curves and damsel-in-distress routine, but he'll see through it eventually, and you'll move on to your next mark. He needs a serious partner if he will have one at all or at least one with enough clout to raise his status, not some attention-seeking little girl."

My mouth gapes open. On one hand, I cannot believe this man's audacity. On the other, he is driving home the same points as Veronica did last night: that I am a silly girl playing in a league she has no business being in.

Before he can insult me further, Ralphie walks in. "Here you go." Feeling the tension in the room, he asks is everything is good.

"Yep," I lie.

"I was getting to know your lady and telling her how hard you've worked in your career."

"Mmm," Ralphie hums. "That's true, I have. It is nice to sit back and have some fun after years of grinding."

I know he doesn't mean it, but the insinuation that I am only 'fun' confirms something in Andre's eyes. As if the words mean, we aren't as serious as he thought. The joke's on him.

"Thank you for getting these. I can show myself out."

As his agent leaves, Ralphie is still watching me suspiciously. "Are you sure you're good?"

"If you can call decaffeinated good," I tease.

That spurs him into action as he hits a few buttons on his fancy coffee machine. I don't know why I didn't tell him about Andre's comments, except that I want to remain in the glow from last night for a while longer before I let another voice into my head.

MY ATTEMPTS at keeping Andre's voice out fail, though. Later that day, as we lay by Ralphie's pool, I can't stop thinking about it. It feeds into the insecurities that surfaced after hearing the WAGs talk about me in the bathroom.

"*Zlatíčko*," the sexy man beside me rasps. "If you don't stop scrunching your face like you ate a lemon, I am going to pull you into this lounger with me, and you will end up with an uneven tan."

"You wouldn't."

But he would. And he does. Leaning over, he grabs me by the waist and pulls me on top of him. I giggle the whole way.

"That's better," he says against my temple, hands splayed over my ass cheeks. "There's that real smile."

"Cheesy," I hum. "What would the world think if they knew big, bad Wreck-It Ralph was secretly a softie?"

"Don't know. Don't care. I am only soft for you."

My heart clenches, knowing that's the truth. To the rest of the world, Radek Nokavik is a big, bad hockey player with a scowl that could scare a baby. But for me, he's sweet. I don't know what I did to deserve the privilege of having him this way.

That thought reignites the spiral of insecurities.

"Tell me," he states.

"Tell you what?"

"Tell me what is making those pretty eyes dim and brow crease."

"It's nothing."

"Morgan," he warns. "Don't make me torture it out of you."

"And how exactly would you do that?"

He pretends to think about it before dawning a mischievous grin as his hands flex on my ass. "I could spank it out of you."

I shiver.

"Or I could tickle it out of you," he suggests, fingers creeping around to my sides. When he digs them in, I squirm and squeal, attempting to escape. In the struggle, we flip positions. Now on top of me, he stares down at me, expression playful but also etched with concern.

"I can't fight your doubts if I don't know them, baby."

Not wanting to expose everything I am processing but desperately wanting his validation, I reach for an easy response. "Do you think I try too hard to get attention? That I need too much?"

Ralphie shifts to knees, giving him a better view of my face. Something must tell him the seriousness of my question.

"As someone who tries to avoid attention, I don't know. I know you always have mine, though. And I wouldn't want it any other way. I can't say if you need too much attention because it's all I can do not to drown you in mine. You're my pretty little houseplant. If I feed you, water you, and show you some love, you flourish. That's all I want for you: to blossom into your true self for the rest of the world the way you do with me."

My eyes prickle at his admission. I slam them shut to stem any tears. I expected him to maybe relieve my concern. I didn't expect him to melt me into a puddle.

Ralphie presses his lips to my closed lids, allowing his words to penetrate. The gesture is tender and short-lived as he moves to pepper my face with kisses.

"Speaking of drowning, I think it's time to go for a swim."

"What?! I wasn't planning to get wet."

"That's too bad, baby."

"Ralph—" a shriek cuts off my chastisement as he lifts me into his arms and jumps into the pool, holding me. When I break the surface of the water, Ralphie is watching me with the full smile that makes my heart tingle. I wrap my body around his and spend the rest of the day reveling in his attention and forgetting everything else.

SIXTEEN

Ralphie

LIFE WITH MORGAN has settled in nicely. The Crush are off to a great start in the season, and I am playing better than ever. After initially learning about her, Andre tried to convince me that a relationship would be a distraction and that this was a 'crucial year in my career.' If anything, Morgan has been grounding. Having something to focus on other than hockey twenty-four seven has been great for my mental game and kept me from overanalyzing every play when I am off the ice.

Instead, I spend that time between Morgan's thighs. Who can think about forechecks when your girl is falling apart against your tongue?

As much as I enjoy our physical connection, I love the emotional one even more. Having her around brings me peace that I didn't know I was missing. I would spend a million nights on the couch watching her crochet mini aliens and kittens. Lately, she's been working on beanies for Tabby and me.

I'm glad the two women connected. I get the impression that most of Morgan's friendships are surface-level. It took a few times hanging out for her to buy into Tabby's genuine affection and enthusiasm, but she is flourishing with a true friend by her side. I also think it helps that the friend has several hockey seasons under her belt. As Fitz college sweetheart, Tabby has been through it all.

The girls got together at Fitz's to watch our first away game. As much as I love knowing she is having fun, I hate that I don't have her greeting me postgame. Not that she has been to many more Crush games. She has only come to one other game and opted to sit in the stands with her brother's girlfriend. Andre has been harping on me to get her back into the suite for 'appearances,' but I don't want her there if it makes her uncomfortable.

After a grueling road win in Baltimore, I trudge into my hotel room, shrugging off my suit jacket as soon as I enter. With a heavy sigh, I walk toward the bathroom to get ready for bed before calling my girl. Saucy minx has been sending me naughty texts all day.

As I flick on the light, I glance in the mirror, where I am met with an unwelcome sight: a naked woman stretched across my pillows.

"Who the fuck are you?" I bellow.

"Ashley," she purrs, sitting up on her knees.

"You need to leave. Now!"

"You don't mean that." She trails her hands up her exposed body before toying with her breasts.

"I can assure you, I do."

Realizing I'm in over my head, I grab my phone and dial the front desk. As much of an asshole as I am, I won't physically throw a naked woman in the hall. That's a job for security.

"Hello? Yes, this is room 7235. There is an intruder in my room. I need her removed immediately. I don't know how she knew what room was mine or how she got in here, but I need that rectified. Thank you."

"Come on, Ralphie," she pouts. "I'll let you wreck me however you want. He told me what you like."

"Don't call me that," I bite out. Hearing Morgan's nickname coming from someone else's lips makes my stomach churn. No one gets to call me that but her. I don't have time to ask who 'he' is because security arrives at the same time a few of my teammates are headed into their rooms. Danvers and Mikelson watch the scene unfold.

Ashley, haphazardly dressed in a robe, screams and fights as they drag her down the hall. Mikelson looks amused, while Danvers is pensive.

"Waiting for you in your room?" Mikelson questions.

"Yeah," I sigh, exasperated.

"But you have Morgan," our goalie states matter-of-factly. "It was all over social media."

I took Morgan to a charity function last weekend, and pictures of us exploded all over the internet. It is the first time I've been seen publicly with a woman. They followed us to brunch the next morning, and I had some colorful words with the paparazzi. They still photographed us, but they maintained a respectable distance. Apparently, pictures of me watching my girlfriend eat an omelet are hot sellers.

Morgan was anxious about it at first, but fucking her against my living room windows that overlook the beach was enough to convince her I didn't give a fuck who knew about us. She is planning our "hard launch" as soon as I return now that she has told her family about us.

"That's probably why he got Naked Manned. Now that they know it's possible to land on his arm or in his bed, all bets are off."

"What's the Naked Man?" Danvers asks. I don't get the reference either, but I don't care at this point.

"You two are helpless," Mikelson huffs when he sees my lack of recognition.

"That's rude," Danvers grumbles.

"It is," I reply. "I'm going to call my girl before she hears about this somewhere else. See you on the bus tomorrow."

Back in my room, I click on Morgan's contact and settle into bed as the video call connects. She looks beautiful in a t-shirt falling off one shoulder and no makeup. Knowing she is comfortable enough to be on video with me when dressed down fills my chest with pride.

"Hi, baby."

"Hi." She beams. "You played amazing tonight."

"Thank you. Did you have fun with Tabby?"

"Yeah, she's a little crazy, but in the best way. She's already planning a trip for the four of us postseason. I told her that was premature, but she ignored me."

"Let her plan. We can always change the details later. It will all depend on how far we get in the playoffs anyway."

"You're going all the way. My psychic told me."

"I'm glad you're confident." As much as I'm enjoying the carefree conversation, I know I need to break the news of my intruder before it hits the media. I hope security will be discreet, but the way the woman was screaming my name all but guarantees some story will hit the internet, and I need to get ahead of it.

"There is something I need to tell you."

"What's that?" she asks apprehensively.

"When I got to my room tonight, someone was in it."

"They gave someone else your room?"

"Not exactly." Even though I did nothing wrong, this is harder to admit than I thought. I might as well rip off the Band-Aid. "There was a woman. A naked woman who had broken into my room to wait for me." My heart clenches at the way her face drops.

"I had her removed immediately, but I wanted to tell you before the story or some version of it got picked up anywhere."

She worries her bottom lip as she searches my face for deceit. She won't find any. I've never lied to her and don't plan to start today.

"Does this happen often?"

"First time for me, but it has happened to a few other guys at one time or another."

"This woman showed up in your room and assumed you'd fuck her?" I can see hurt in her eyes, but her tone is schooled. "Why would she think that if it wasn't something you've done before?"

"She was delusional. No sane person breaks into a stranger's hotel room and thinks anything but trespassing charges will happen. You have nothing to worry about, *Zlatíčko*. No one exists in my world but you."

Her shoulders drop at my admission. "Sorry," she mutters.

"It's okay. One day, you'll trust me implicitly. Until then, I'll be right here reassuring you of my devotion." That melts away her remaining doubt. We spend the next hour talking about her evening with Tabby and the crazy bachelorette party she served at Two-One-Oh last night. By the time the call ends, I'm counting the minutes until I'm wheels down in LA with my girl.

As I lay down to sleep, I wonder how Ashley knew which room was mine. Only a select group of personnel have access to the team's room numbers, and the list of those who can request access is even smaller. I am inclined to think it is an inside job by the hotel, but the way she said, 'He told her what I like,' is weird.

SEVENTEEN

Morgan

THE INCIDENT with Ralphie's 'Naked Nancy,' as Tabby calls it, rattled me more than I let on. I know if he wanted to cheat, he could, but the reality of how easy it would be for him leaves me unsettled. I'm not surprised people are throwing themselves at him. I'm highly suspicious that everyone who sees him wants him. He has that 'don't fuck with me' vibe and BDE that ruins my panties. It's not a stretch that other women would want a taste.

I see the way people sneak peeks when he visits me at Clamatis or on the rare occasion we go out to dinner. They don't think I'm enough for him. He should be with a model or actress, not a 'wannabe social climber,' as one gossip channel kindly put it.

Even if I wanted to avoid the mean things they say, it's hard to do when they tag me. My comment section has been brutal the past few weeks. On the plus side, I had a brand I have been trying to work with for months finally get back to me. I know they only want me now because I'm connected to an NHL superstar, but I am not dumb enough to pass up an opportunity due to pride. I'll prove my worth with the content I create.

It doesn't help that the hate is also coming from those close to him. Andre's digs, whenever Ralphie can't hear, are not missed. Neither are the long calls that just happen to coincide with the times our schedules align or the stressing Ralphie out about the importance of his performance this season. The man is getting under my skin. He wants me to throw in the towel, but I won't.

Ralphie treats me better than anyone ever has, and I am not going to give that up easily. I've been tempted to tell him what his agent has been saying, but I don't want to add more to his plate. He is already working harder than ever with two of the team's top scorers out. He doesn't need the pressure of Andre and me not getting along. Plus, the sneaky agent never does anything that leaves proof of his disrespect. If Andre thinks I'll take his rude behavior out on Ralphie, he's wrong.

It isn't simply the way Ralphie treats me that I love, but he has helped me shift my priorities, too. Not in the selfish, manipulative way Chet did, but by showing my worth. By making nights in with him so much more appealing than partying with 'friends' who only show up when it's convenient.

My social life exploded with the news of my relationship. All of a sudden, I was hearing from people I hadn't talked to in months. Casual friends were now acting as if we were long-lost besties. It's shedding light on my lack of genuine connections outside my family. I never realized how hollow those relationships were until I had something real with Ralphie and Tabby. That pint-sized powerhouse bulldozed her way into my life. Despite not remembering when I agreed, she convinced me to make her a beanie with Fitz's number on it.

She and Ralphie are the same in their overwhelming presence. The man came into my life like a tidal wave. He rushed past my defenses, and I never looked back. It should scare me how quickly he's become my safe place. Despite my desire to be loved, I never let another man get this far under my skin, knowing it would hurt like hell when they left. But with Ralphie, it's different.

His kindness, unceasing support, and praise make me feel almost worthy. He validates my emotions, listens to my ideas, and never looks annoyed when I drone on about my latest project or a crazy passenger interaction. He is genuinely interested in my thoughts and emotions. All I can do is hope it's enough to hook him because I am falling fast.

All of this has put into perspective how I have allowed other people to mistreat me in the past due to my insecurities. Being treated well has given me the confidence to ignore people only interested in me for clout. I deserve better, and it's time I demand better from the people I spend my energy on. Why waste it on self-indulgent takers when there are people in my life who genuinely value me?

Setting down the top I've been working on, I realize it's time to pack for my next flight. I traded with a coworker who wanted to surprise her boyfriend for their anniversary. It should be a quick overnight to Denver and back home tomorrow morning.

Ralphie asked me to attend his game tomorrow night. With no reason not to, I agreed. I'm nervous about facing the WAG firing squad again, but Tabby assured me she would be there. Andre is supposed to attend, too. Yay. Thankfully, he will be in a different suite.

Speak of the devil, and by the devil, I mean Andre; an email notification pops onto my screen as I confirm my travel details. Blowing out a raspberry, I hit open.

Ms. Becker,

Attached you will find yet another article bringing negative attention to Radek. Neither he nor the public need to be subjected to pictures of you hanging over Kings players. I don't care about your image, but I do care about his. If you could *try* to play the part of doting girlfriend at tomorrow's game, that would be much appreciated.

Though I've never had to tell a grown woman how to dress before, Radek does not want to be embarrassed. Please wear the correct jersey and pair it with whatever you deem appropriate as long as it isn't too attention-seeking. The more subtle, the better. I would prefer any team material be licensed by the league and not homemade. I think we can all agree you've gotten enough attention lately.

The Crush are doing great in the division standing, and we want all press coming from tomorrow's game to be about Radek's performance, not what his girlfriend was wearing or any antics she gets up to.

Please be on your best behavior,

Andre Svoboda

SVBD Management

I know I shouldn't let his words get to me, but they are a kick to the gut. The email is written in a professional tone, but I can sense the underlying snark. The attention-seeking comment hits particularly hard. It isn't the first time I've been called that. I love sparkling things. I know my height, blonde hair, and generous rack attract stares, but I can't help that. I don't want to hide myself and not wear things I enjoy because of it.

Sure, my clothes and overall appearance used to be a tool I utilized to catch men's eyes and fit into the circles I wanted to be a part of. But at the end of the day, I like who I am and how I look. I like *me*. It's taken me a long time and generous reassurance from Ralphie to come to that conclusion, but I do.

I won't dim my light for Andre or even Ralphie. I was under the impression Ralphie would never want me to. Was I wrong? This message is pure Andre, but he mentioned wearing the 'correct' jersey. Did Ralphie tell Andre about the first game I attended when I didn't wear his name?

The email also said *Ralphie* didn't want to be embarrassed, not Andre. Have I embarrassed him at past games? I know the first one was a toss-up, but I thought the other with Carina went much better. I ended up on the jumbotron a couple of times, but I don't think I did anything that would embarrass anyone except myself. In my defense, they can't put me on the snack cam and not expect me to house my hotdog.

Shame roils in my stomach before I shut it down. Since being with Ralphie, I have become more and more assured of myself. I won't let one email from a jackhole undue all the internal work I've done. I'll talk to Ralphie about all this tomorrow after his game. I should have come clean to him about Andre's comments a while ago, but better late than never.

And if he agrees with his agent, I don't know what I'll do, but he's never given me an indication that he does. I'm going to hold on to believing his actions until his words tell me otherwise.

EIGHTEEN

Morgan

PULLING UP TO MY APARTMENT, I sigh in relief. The last twenty-four hours have been some of the craziest in my entire career. Weather delays last night kept us from leaving until three hours after our scheduled flight time.

We arrived in Denver after midnight, and I crashed until 5 a.m. when I had to get ready for my 8 a.m. return flight. I should have made it back by ten at the latest, but mechanical delays and a missing copilot grounded us for hours. It's right after three when I get home. I desperately need to shower and nap before Ralphie's game, but my brain is fried.

Not only was the flight delayed and full of turbulence, but the passengers were a nightmare. We almost had to request one be removed before takeoff when she loudly insisted another passenger trade seats with her so she could sit by her husband. She was not happy when that person refused to give up their sixth-row aisle seat for a middle seat on the twenty-eighth row.

The last thing I want is to dress up and be around more people. I would much rather curl up on my couch. All my rage-induced confidence after reading Andre's email has fizzled out with my energy level. I do not have it in me to face him and the other WAGs tonight.

It's been days since I've seen Ralphie, but being in the suite isn't that different from watching from home. I don't see him until after either way. I know he wanted me to go, but surely he'll understand I'm not up for it.

3:16 PM

ME

Finally made it home.

RALPHIE

Did you get much sleep?

ME

No. Since they kept telling us the plane was almost ready, there was no time to nap in the lounge. I'm running on four hours.

RALPHIE

You must be exhausted. You should nap.

ME

I'm about to, but I am beat. It was a madhouse on the flight today. Are you at the stadium yet?

The puck drops at seven. And his rigorous pregame routine requires a serious time investment.

RALPHIE

I'm here. I dropped a jersey off with Madison so you can wear mine this time and not some other fucker's.

I tense at the reference. I had hoped the correct jersey comment was just Andre finding something to pick at. It must still be bothering Ralphie if he would drive across town on a game day to drop one off.

My desire to go tonight plummets further at the idea Ralphie could share sentiments with Andre.

ME

> About that, I was thinking about watching from home. Getting glammed up sounds terrible right now.

RALPHIE

> Your name is already on the list. You don't have to get dressed up. Just throw on my jersey and your beanie.

The unlicensed, homemade beanie your agent specifically asked me not to wear? Fat chance.

ME

> No way! That's what I wore the last time I was there. They would totally notice. I don't want to embarrass you.

RALPHIE

> You could never embarrass me.

I have an email in my inbox that would beg to differ.

ME

> Will you get in trouble if my name is on the list and I don't go? I am not up for faking happy tonight.

RALPHIE

> You never have to fake your feelings, Zlatíčko.

> I won't try to convince you if you don't want to go. Andre may get on my ass about it, but he can shove it. I pay him, not the other way around.

I bet he will be thrilled I'm not there. There is no risk of embarrassment. Although, I'm sure he'll find a way to complain about how it makes me appear as an unsupportive girlfriend or some other dumb take.

I get the vibe that Ralphie is disappointed with my decision, but I am beyond relieved. After the email and everything I went through traveling the past day, I need a night to decompress. All I want is a quick shower and to sleep.

That plan is interrupted by Madison hogging the bathroom. As I'm deciding between going straight to sleep or waiting it out, she emerges surrounded by steam. Great, there went all the hot water.

"You're home," she notes.

"Yeah." My reply comes out more snarky than intended, the lack of sleep and a grueling day getting to me. My mood plummets even further knowing my shower will be lukewarm at best.

"Geez, what crawled up your ass."

"Are you done in the bathroom? I need to wash the plane off me before I crash."

"I have a few more things to do, but I guess if you're quick, I can wait."

By a few more things, she means she'll spend an absorbent amount of time doing her hair and makeup only to restart halfway through.

"How generous of you," I snap.

"Not all of us have loaded hockey player Sugar Daddies as a backup. I gotta pull out all the stops if I want free drinks."

"Are you kidding me? He is not my 'Sugar Daddy.' Why would you even say that?"

"Could've fooled me. The man bought you jewelry on your first date and dropped off another gift this afternoon. It's on your bed, in case you were wondering. I don't know when I became your secretary, but that isn't what I signed up for when I agreed to be your roommate."

I stand there slack-jawed at her audacity. We've never been besties, but we are friends. At least, I thought we were. We've been perfectly compatible roommates up until this point. I let her use my car when hers crapped out for Chrissake.

Her jab about Ralphie spending money on me is ridiculous. He isn't paying any of my bills. But even if he were, that wouldn't be her business. Plus, it's not as if she's destitute. Working for the airline may be her only job, but she makes decent money. And I don't recall her turning down all the dinners at Nobu she enjoyed during her brief fling with that former child star turned cult leader.

I don't know if it's because I'm tired from my hellish day or years of built-up tension from being walked over by other people, but I snap.

"First of all, the necklace he bought me cost sixty dollars. Even the brokeass men you date could afford that. Second, I don't know where this hate is coming from, but I don't appreciate it. I have been nothing but a good friend to you since we met, which is more than I can say for you. You abandoned me when I got sick a few weeks ago. I would never do that to you."

"Your boyfriend was here."

"You were planning to leave before he arrived, and we both know it." Her lack of response is enough of an answer.

"I don't know if you're jealous or hormonal or simply being a bitch, but I don't appreciate you talking down to me as if I'm using a man to get ahead. I work hard for everything I have. If my boyfriend wants to give me his *jersey*—" I put extra emphasis on that to show how ridiculous she's being "—it's none of your business. Hell, if he wants to give me a Ferrari, it's none of your business and in no way detracts from how I've supported myself up to this point."

Now it's Madison's turn to be shocked. I've never talked to her this way before. Hell, I don't know if I've ever truly stood up for myself to anyone other than Chet. It is incredible. Is this how Rob feels when he calls out Dad's disapproval? It's exhilarating. I need to do this more.

"If you'll excuse me," I say as I push past her. "I'm going to rinse off before crawling into bed to sleep off my crappy trip. Since I am sure you used up all the hot water, I'll be quick."

As I rinse off, a million snarky comments run through my head. Wanting to take the high road, I don't repeat any of them. Instead, I make quick work in the shower and fall asleep the second my head hits the pillow.

NINETEEN

Ralphie

ANDRE GAVE me an earful about Morgan missing today's game. I don't know why he cares whether or not she is here, but his constant harping on her is grating my nerves. Only a handful of partners are at every game. Morgan has a job and life. She can't always drop everything to be here. If I don't care, why does he?

Annoyance sits heavy in my chest as I wrap my stick for today's game, partly due to Andre's latest lecture but also because we're playing our division rivals.

"You good?" Fitz asks as I rip off the tape and start over.

"Yeah," I grunt.

"Tabby told me Morgan isn't coming. Everything okay there?"

"Fine. She had a rough flight and wants to take it easy at home."

"Gotcha. The girls can get together another time. Tabby will have to terrorize Veronica by herself."

I smirk. Veronica may be the wife of our captain, but she is a stuck-up bitch. She thinks bagging a number one draft pick eight years ago makes her queen of the team. Most of us have nothing to do with her or the WAG activities, but I kept my distance after how she treated Morgan. Knowing Morgan doesn't have to deal with her negative energy tonight does lighten my mood slightly.

The tension in the air is palpable during the anthem. We've always had a tumultuous relationship with Vegas. One of their defensemen, Kragers, always plays this side of too rough and hardly ever gets called. The two of us are evenly matched in stature, but I'm faster, which grinds his gears.

The weight of his gaze rests on me during warmups and the pregame ceremony. Since we're both starters, we match up on the ice for the puck drop.

"Heard you got a hot new piece," he jeers as we wait for the ref's signal.

"Watch it," I growl, voice laced with a warning he doesn't heed. He's never had anything he can use to rile me up until Morgan.

"The guys and I plan on heading to the club she works to celebrate after we win. I heard they have special body shots. I can't wait to see for myself."

That's all it takes for me to get in his face. Logically, I know Morgan isn't working tonight or even do body shots, but the idea of him being near her makes my blood boil.

"Fuck. Off," I seethe.

"That's not what she'll be saying later."

I move to jostle him, but he jets off. The bastard distracted me from the start of the game. His team has the puck, and I'm stuck playing catch-up.

They manage to score, but several possessions later, so do we. We head into the second period, tied 1-1. Similar to the previous puck drop, Kragers is in my face talking shit. This time, I ignore him, which pisses him off more. Racing down the ice with the puck, I pass to Connor right as Krager slams me into the boards hard. He should be called for cross-checking, but the referees don't see it. Fans are booing as my coach yells from the bench at the missed call.

Shaking him off, I go after the puck and try to make a play. Vegas regains possession and barrels toward Danvers, only to be cut off by Mikelson. The puck is passed to Troy and set up for a shot at Vegas' goal. Realizing I'm about to outrun him, Krager grabs my jersey in a blatant hold and throws me to the ground.

I pop back up to assist my teammates, but he is all over me again. He checks me into the boards a second time. As we scramble for the puck, he continues his earlier shit-talking.

When his words don't have the desired impact, he pulls out his dirty tricks, hoping he won't get called. I'm ready for his antics and fight back just as hard. Connor and one of Vegas' other defensive players join the scuffle, and my helmet gets knocked off as we fight for possession.

I knock the puck through everyone's legs, hoping it makes it back to Troy, but before I can see if it does, everything goes dark.

TWENTY

DESPITE HOW MANY times I watch Ralphie play, I still haven't gotten used to the fighting. I don't know if I am overly sensitive from the last few days or if the game is rougher than usual, but I am on pins and needles watching Ralphie and another player face off.

They have been in each other's faces since the puck dropped and haven't let up. It's near the end of the second period, and the pair are pressed into the boards, fighting for the puck. I sigh in relief when another Crush player joins, but they are quickly met by someone else from Vegas.

I watch as Ralphie's helmet flies off at the exact moment the puck flies out of the fray. Instead of ending the fight, though, the opposing player brings up his stick and hits Ralphie in the head.

My heart stutters as everyone freezes on the ice. When Ralphie hits the ground, all hell breaks loose. Connor pushes the offending player away from Ralphie as players from both teams barrel toward the action, dropping their gloves on the way. As a fistfight ensues, refs struggle to break it up as they signal for the medic team to come onto the ice.

I hold my breath as they load Ralphie onto a gurney and whisk him back to the locker room or wherever the hell they take injured players. My heart beats wildly in my chest as I consider my next move. If I had gone to the game, I could go down and see him, but I don't know what to do now.

He wasn't moving or seemingly conscious the last time he was shown on the screen. The ice was engulfed in chaos, but I heard the announcers state his status as unknown. He has to be okay, right? Hockey is dangerous, but it isn't life or death. At least, it isn't supposed to be.

Jolting from my spot on the couch, I scramble to get on my shoes and grab my keys. As I run out my door, I realize I don't know where to go. Getting to the stadium at this time of night will take forever, and for all I know, they're sending him to the hospital. My frantic Googling of 'what happens when hockey players pass out' is interrupted by a call from Tabby.

"Morgan, did you see?"

"Yes! Is he okay? Have you heard anything? Is he still there?"

"Take a breath, girl. They're taking him to USC Medical Center. That's where I work. I'll meet you there."

"Is he awake?" My voice cracks as I ask.

"I don't know. But he'll be okay. The team doctors are fantastic."

I ARRIVE at the hospital in a panic. After driving in circles for fifteen minutes to find parking, my hackles rise as Veronica's unwelcome face greets me in the waiting room.

"What are you doing here?" I ask.

"I'm the captain's wife. It's my job to ensure all the players are cared for, especially when they don't have partners or family nearby."

"He has a partner."

"So you say. I'm honestly surprised you made it. Since I didn't see you at the game, I assumed you were gallivanting across the midwest or serving shots to B-list actors."

I am momentarily shocked by her outright vitriol. I don't know what has made her turn from passive to cruel, but I do not have time for her mean-girl antics.

"I don't know what your problem is with me, nor do I care. I am in a relationship with Ralphie. Not the Crush. Not you. How I spend my free time is not anyone's business but his. I am not going to let your bitchy attitude influence how I spend it.

"I understand your apprehension of letting a new girl into your little club, especially one that doesn't fit your mold. But I also don't care. I am here because my man is hurt, and no one is going to stop me from checking on him, least of all you."

Her mouth gapes open, but my worry over Ralphie supersedes my ability to enjoy the sight. "If you'll excuse me, I have more important things to do than defend myself to a wannabe First Lady, pick me girl."

With that, I turn on my heel and search for the trauma unit. I finally reach the right place, only to be stopped by the charge nurse.

"What do you mean you can't confirm or deny if Radek Nokavik is awake?!"

"Exactly what I said, ma'am," the nurse calmly explains. "We are only allowed to update next of kin on a patient's status."

"Can I see him?"

"Unfortunately, we can't allow anyone to see him who isn't on the team's approved visitors list."

"But I'm his girlfriend," I argue.

"You might be, but there isn't a way to prove that for sure or that he would want you here."

"He doesn't want me here?"

"That isn't what she's saying," a familiar voice interrupts. Turning, Tabby engulfs me in a hug. "Hi, Mary."

"Tabitha, what are you doing here on your off day?"

"I came to check on Radek. I believe I'm on the approved list?"

"You are?" Mary and I say at the same time.

"Yep. His agent is the emergency contact, but he isn't always available. Considering his friends are all on the team and still playing, that leaves me. It helps that I'm a nurse, too." She runs a soothing hand down my arm and addresses me directly. "I'm sure he will switch it to you after this."

Mary studies us both apprehensively. "I was told specifically not to let Ms. Becker through."

"By who?"

"Mr. Svoboda."

Fucking Andre. Why would he want to keep me away from Ralphie, especially when he's injured?

"I understand," Tabby replies.

"You do?" My mouth parts, shocked my friend isn't taking my side. The wide eyes she shoots be silent further protests.

"Of course, she is not going to tell you where Ralphie is. But she is going to tell me. If you happen to follow me to the room, there is nothing she can do about it. Right, Mary?"

"Absolutely. As his backup emergency contact, Tabby has every right to visit Mr. Nokavik in 802."

When we reach his room, we hear raised voices from the other side. I move to enter, but Tabby stops me.

"Wait. This sounds important."

"Who is it?"

"One guess," she replies with a scrunch of her nose. Andre, of course. Pushing the handle lightly, she cracks the door enough for us to hear an epic blowout where Andre all but admits to not only sending a naked woman to Ralphie's hotel room but also planting stories about me in the press.

Ralphie may have thought he shielded me from the tabloid hit pieces, but I saw them. They didn't affect me nearly as much as the shit going on in my own head. I let him think I didn't know about them because the way he tried to protect me from them made me realize how deeply I love him.

I've never been in love before. I thought I loved my high school boyfriend. I said I loved the guy I dated for six months when I was twenty, but none of my past relationships compare to what I feel for Ralphie. His devotion and care split my heart and put it back together every day. I know we haven't been together long, but there is nothing I wouldn't do for this man, including putting up with a lifetime of his slimy agent, but it sounds like I won't have to.

When things get too heated, Tabby charges in like the boss bitch she is. Andre storms out, but my gaze is locked on Ralphie. He looks both fragile and mighty in his hospital gown. All I want to do is go to him, but I'm afraid of making his injuries worse.

He says something to me, but my mind replays seeing him hit the ice. When I can't take the visual anymore, I slam my eyes shut and whisper, "You got hurt."

TWENTY-ONE

Ralphie

A THROBBING HEAD and aching body greet me as I wake up. "Bright," I rasp.

I let out a sigh of relief as the lights dim. "Welcome back," Andre's familiar voice says. "You gave us quite the scare."

"Where is Morgan?"

"Don't worry about that right now. Worry about resting up. Kragen gave you one hell of a wallop. I imagine he will be suspended for several games. Shameful to slash a player when his helmet is off."

"He slashed me?" What an asshat.

"Right on the back of the skull. Knocked you out cold. The doctors think it's only a grade-three concussion. All in all, it could be worse."

"Where is Morgan?" I repeat.

"So worried about the bimbo," I think he mutters under his breath. My eyes shoot open wide at that.

"What the fuck did you say?"

"Nothing. What was Krager chirping about to rile you up at the beginning of the match? You were more aggressive than usual."

"He was talking shit about my girl." I lose my composure when his face twists in disgust. "What is your deal? Do you have a problem with Morgan? Is that why she isn't here?"

That question makes him nervous. "I don't have a problem with her per se. I wish if you were going to get into that kind of relationship, you would have let me help pick someone more suitable."

"That 'kind of relationship?' What are you talking about? Morgan isn't a 'kind of' anything. She's the woman I love and plan to spend the rest of my life with. I'm going to ask her to move in with me after the season ends."

"Don't say that," he groans. "If I would have realized you were in this deep, I would have taken more drastic measures. We need to get her to sign an NDA. Do not move her in with you without letting me draw a contract up first to protect your assets. Though, I'm sure a few months of seeing her before she dolls up for the day will knock some sense into you. It's never as glamorous behind the curtain."

Am I more concussed than I think? Surely, he isn't saying what I think he's saying. He sounds like the exact flavor of asshole who hurt her self-esteem. And what does he mean by drastic measures?

Suddenly, everything clicks in my head. "Did you send that woman to my room in Baltimore?"

"'Send' is a strong word. I might have procured a key but didn't lead her there myself."

"You practically did!" With that tidbit of information, more thoughts unlock.

"And are you the reason we've been followed lately and hit pieces about Morgan are popping up in those rags?"

Though I've done my best to distract her, articles about Morgan have been rampant in the LA gossip magazines the past two weeks. They've spanned from completely off-base speculation to interviews with old "boyfriends" calling her names or saying that she cheated on them with me. I suspect our buddy Chet is responsible for that last one.

When he doesn't answer, I know I hit the nail on the head.

"Why would you do that? I have been a model client for you since day one!"

"Exactly! And ever since *she* came into your life, you've changed.

You hid her from me when you first got together, you're chummier with your teammates, and you're out on the town, visiting her at that club."

"You're mad that I'm happy?" My head hurts way too much to be having this conversation right now.

"You're not following the plan."

"What plan? You're the one who wanted me in a relationship, so I looked committed to LA."

"Committed but not rooted down," he counters. "I wanted you to get with someone high profile who could elevate your status beyond the league. It would have led to more endorsements and forced the Crush to up their offer to ensure you didn't end up signing elsewhere. Your payday would have been huge."

"You mean is, YOUR payday would be huge."

"Tomato, to-mah-to."

"How about 'Tomato, you're fired.'"

"What?" He pales. "You can't fire me. You're in no mental state to do that."

"I can, and I did. If I need to tell you again in a few days, I will. But get the hell out of my hospital room. I need to find my phone and call my girl. She's gotta be worried sick."

"No need," Tabby declares as she charges in. A stricken Morgan trails behind her. She freezes as she stares through Andre and takes me in.

"This is all your fault," he seethes at her.

"Get. Out," I growl. With one final, hateful glare, he leaves the room. I rub my temples. Arguing was not the best thing to do for my headache, but it had to be done. The motion spurs Tabby into action. She fiddles with the monitors before grabbing my chart to read over. Morgan stays rooted in place.

"Come here, baby," I coo. I may be injured, but that won't stop me from taking care of her. She appears to need to lay down as much as I do.

"You got hurt," she whispers, ignoring however much of the fight with Andre she overheard.

"I did. But I'm okay now," I assure her.

"He is," Tabby chimes in. "All his tests came back clear, but they're keeping him overnight for observation."

"I saw them wheel you off the ice," Morgan replies as if she didn't hear either of us. The tremble of her bottom lip makes me want to jump out of this bed to comfort her, but one glance at Tabby tells me she won't let me do that.

"*Zlatičko*," I say with as much force as possible without hurting my head further. "Come closer. I want to touch you, and you can see for yourself that I'm okay."

She takes one tentative step forward before breaking out of her trance and scurrying onto the bed. The tension leftover from my argument with Andre seeps out of my body as I hold her in my arms.

"I'll give you two some privacy and shoot the guys an update," Tabby whispers.

I nod in thanks, not taking my eyes off Morgan. I shift until her torso is pressed against my chest, hips between my legs. I run a soothing hand up and down her back as she soaks my gown with her tears. When her sobs turn into sniffles, I kiss the top of her head gently.

"What?" I ask as she murmurs something I can't understand against my chest.

Leaning onto her elbows, she meets my gaze. "I love you."

A wide grin breaks out across my face. "Who knew getting bashed in the head is all it would take to get you to admit your feelings for me."

"Not funny!"

"It's a little funny. And I love you, too." Leaning down as much as the position allows, I gently press my lips into hers. I want to devour her whole, but my throbbing head puts the brakes on that.

The fact is, I've been trying to figure out how to express my love for her for a while, but it always seemed too soon or the wrong moment to tell her. Now that she's pulled the trigger, I want to use every breath to tell her how much I care.

"You enchanted me from that very first night, and I've never been the same. Every moment we're together is the best of my life, and every minute we're apart, I am counting down until you're back in my arms."

"That's way more poetic than my tearful 'I love you,'" she grumbles.

Laughing, I give her one more chaste kiss before guiding her head back to my chest. When her adrenaline wears off, she sleeps soundly in my arms. She doesn't even stir when the doctors check on me or when the guys finally make it to the hospital.

Despite the fogginess of my head, everything is right with the world.

TWENTY-TWO

Morgan

"ARE you sure you're ready for this? We can wait until Christmas," I say when Ralphie pulls up to my family home, knowing full well that if Mom has off Thanksgiving, she won't get Christmas.

"I face off against two-hundred-pound men every day, *Zlatíčko*. I think I can handle dinner with your parents."

"You underestimate how protective my dad and brother can be."

"Anyone who loves and cares for you is an ally in my book."

Heaving out a sigh, I wait for Ralphie to let me out of the car. It's only been one week since he passed the concussion protocol, but he insisted we join my family for Thanksgiving. He even got tickets for my dad and brother to go with me to tomorrow's game against Houston.

The past few weeks have been a whirlwind. After the hospital released him, the team doctors ran several tests on him before allowing him to set foot back in the stadium, let alone on the ice. On top of that, he had to meet with his attorney to finalize severing ties with Andre.

More negative stories came out about us before we sent a cease and desist letter to all parties involved. That shut everyone up for the time being, including those mystery articles claiming to be lovers from our pasts.

I did read one interesting article about a washed-up sports agent begging his final client to stick with him at a swanky downtown restaurant. I made sure to forward it to Andre and remind him people don't like 'attention-seeking' behavior. Was it petty? Yes. Satisfying? Incredibly.

While Ralphie recovered, I took vacation days I had banked with the airlines and worked as few shifts at the clubs as I could get away with. Ralphie insisted he needed me there to take care of him, but he did more caring for me than the other way around. I would have called him out on using his injury as an excuse to get me to stay with him, but I loved it as much as he did.

After my showdown with Madison, things were icy at first. The distance has helped. I haven't been home more than a few hours at a time in the last week. I woke up to a text from her on Tuesday apologizing for her behavior. She and her boyfriend were on the outs, and she took her emotions out on me, jealous that I was happy. Things have calmed down between them, and she and I are mostly back to normal.

I would have loved more time holed up with my man, but I cherish holidays with my family, especially now that my brother lives fifteen hundred miles away. Rob is back in California for Thanksgiving, but when Carina's Christmas break hits, he'll spend the time with her in Memphis. The season may have recently ended, but spring training will be here before we know it.

Carrying the casserole and pie I made for the meal, Ralphie trails behind me with his contribution of wine and beer. I explained that he didn't need to bring anything, but he brushed me off.

"Are you sure you aren't nervous?" I ask before opening the door to my parents' house.

"Not at all. The way I see it, meeting your parents is the last obstacle in finally convincing you to move in with me."

"I am not moving in with you," I reiterate for the one-hundredth time.

"We'll see."

EPILOGUE

Ralphie

STANDING IN THE LIVING ROOM, I watch Morgan in the pool with our dog, Max. It took six months, but I finally enticed my girl to move in with me under the guise of taking care of the pup. I had to fib and say it was a lifelong dream to be a dog owner, but I don't regret my lie two and a half years later.

I smile as she tries to coax the Augie into the water with her.

"Nokavik, are you listening to me?" Tanner, my new agent, asks.

"Kind of," I admit.

"So you heard what I said about being traded?"

"I heard you," I sigh. I knew this was coming but hoped it wouldn't. With many of my former draft mates retired, I'm among the team's oldest and most expensive players. After a disappointing season, the team is looking to add young blood to the roster. My salary would pay for three or four rookies and overseas players. To free up cap space, they'll send me to a team hoping for an experienced all-star to help clinch the cup. It's not the worst thing to happen, but I hate change.

"What frozen hellscape am I going to?" I ask, defeated.

"That's the good news. You're going to the Sunshine State. The Tampa Thunder are excited to have you."

Tampa? I can work with Tampa. Morgan will move with me wherever I go, but convincing her to move to Milwaukee or Winnipeg would have been a tough sell. Thankfully, it's the offseason, giving us time to find a place and move without working around a busy playing schedule. There is one thing I need to do before I break the news to my girl.

"WHAT ARE WE DOING HERE?" Morgan asks as we pull up to the familiar cafe. "I thought we were meeting Fitz and Tabby."

"We are, but Tabby is craving the sausage and Monterrey kolache. I told Fitz we'd pick it up on the way."

Morgan nods as if her friend's pregnancy craving is the most normal thing in the world. Tabby is four months pregnant with their second child, and Morgan has been working hard on a blanket and hockey skate booties for the little boy.

I lead us on to the deck near the takeout window, but instead of placing an order, we walk over to the other side, which is adorned with flowers and string lights. This is out of character for the mom-and-pop shop that upgraded from a food truck years ago.

The cafe may be basic, but it was the second-best investment I ever made. The first sits heavy in my pocket.

Taking in the scene, Morgan turns to me, confusion across her angelic face. The way her bronze skin and blonde hair shimmer in the sunset light consume my thoughts, and I almost forget the reason we are here.

When I remember, I slowly lower myself onto one knee and wait for her to peer back in my direction. I almost laugh at the shocked expression she wears when she does.

"Morgan, these last three years with you have been nothing short of incredible. Your sunny disposition brightened my darkest days. You opened me up to new experiences and gave me a life I never dreamt I'd lead. I want to spend every day I have left on this earth making your life as magical as you've made mine. Will you give me that opportunity and the honor of calling you my wife?"

Tears pool in her ocean-blue eyes as she takes a stuttering breath. She shakes her head back and forth as if she can't believe this is happening before realizing the mixed message.

"Yes," she exclaims, hands clutching each other in front of her chest. "Of course, I'll marry you."

"Even if it means you'll have to leave LA?"

"I'd follow you to Timbuktu."

Rising, I pull her face into mine and sink into the kind of kiss we've shared a million times. This time, though, we kiss with new adventures looming on the horizon.

When I finally pull away, I grab her hand and slide on the ring. It's over the top, but so is my girl. She hits me with her genuine smile as she stares at the four-carat oval diamond surrounded by a halo of smaller stones. Transfixed on her new bling, she doesn't notice the cafe doors sliding open beside her.

Streaming outside, we're both engulfed in hugs by our loved ones. Morgan laughs as she embraces her mom and Tabby. Her dad, Frank, pats me on the back. We've come a long way from the cold shoulder he offered on our first meeting. He swore me to secrecy, but he teared up when I asked for his daughter's hand.

"I can't believe you did this!" my girl cries, surveying the love surrounding us.

"I have one more surprise," I admit. "Do you think you can handle it?"

"I don't know, but let's find out."

Giving the signal, the last guest joins our party.

"BOBERT!" she shouts at the tall man who wraps his arms around her. In the three years I've known Rob, he's changed a lot. He's no longer the scraggly starry-eyed rookie. He's filled out and matured a hell of a lot. Losing the love of your life can do that.

He's made the most of it and has quickly become one of the top pitchers in the MLB since being called up last season. That may be a silver lining in his suffering, but having what I have with Morgan, I know it isn't worth the trade. Hopefully, he'll discover that sooner rather than later. I hate seeing the dull emotions behind his eyes. He doesn't have Morgan's sparkle, but he lost some of his playful spirit after Carina left.

Letting go of her brother, my future bride barrels into me. "Thank you," she whispers against my neck.

"Anything for you, *Zlatíčko*. You know that."

Wiping the wetness on her cheeks with my thumbs, I press my lips to hers in a chaste kiss. "Here's to a lifetime of only happy tears."

"Here, here!" our onlookers cheer. It's an impossible promise, but one I'll strive to make true for the rest of our lives.

THANK you for reading Ralphie and Morgan's story. Want more? Visit my website (katsummerswrites.com) for a bonus scene that details Thanksgiving at Morgan's parent's house and their first Christmas together.

You can also catch a glimpse of them three years *after* the epilogue in Robby and Carina's second chance romance, *Behind in the Count*. Read an excerpt from that story on the next page.

BEHIND IN THE COUNT
NASHVILLE SONGBIRDS BOOK ONE

Carina

"I can't believe you sent that guacamole back!" Kim marvels as we show the bouncer our IDs.

"What can I say?" I shrug. "After four years in Cali, my guac standards are high."

She shakes her head. "At least the margaritas were up to Her Majesty's satisfaction. Now, let's go to the bar, do a round of shots, and hit the dancefloor. I am ready to get my groove on."

Downing a shot of Jose and grabbing my tequila sunrise, the girls and I make our way out to the back of the dance floor. I love this place. The vibe at Paula's is unlike anything else. The disco balls make the light play off my silk dress. Was silk the best choice for a club where I will surely get a drink spilled on me and/or sweat on? Doubtful. But Tiffany insisted this was the outfit the universe wanted for me, and who am I to argue when the universe speaks?

The little lilac dress is gorgeous. It's form-fitting at the top but then flares out from my waist until it hits mid-thigh. I am average in the chest area, but the straight cut and tiny straps highlight what I do have well. Combined with the beachy waves in my long brown hair and my signature red lip, I am not ashamed to admit I look damn good tonight.

The DJ is on fire, and we are having a great time. Resident mom friend, Haley, goes to grab us some water since we've all had a few drinks at this point. While she's gone, a pair of guys move closer to us. One is taller with flaming red hair and a baby face. The second one resembles a shorter Tom Selleck since he's rocking the eighties mustache that has become popular as of late. I'm undecided on my take on staches in general, but this guy is not pulling it off.

"Dibs on the ginger," Kim whisper-shouts. I nod at her. Her desire for redheaded babies is well-documented, and I am not about to get in her way. As Kim and her guy dance, his friend puts out his hand, which after a moment of hesitation, I take.

He spins me around until my back is to his front, and we move along with the music. He is a decent dancer, though he seems more preoccupied with smelling my hair than dancing to the beat. Since the club is packed, we don't have much room to move anyway. I peek over at Kim, who gives me a thumbs up.

Midsize PI, as I've dubbed him, breathes directly into my ear and tightens his grip on my hips. "You are fucking hot in this dress, sweet cheeks," he says. Sweet cheeks? Gag.

"Thanks," I murmur, barely loud enough for him to hear.

"It will look better on my bedroom floor later."

I laugh but don't say anything. I told Tiffany I would be more open to finding a guy tonight, but I'm not a hookup kind of girl. There is no chance any of my clothing will be seeing his bedroom floor anytime soon or ever. Plus, he is so not the one.

Not getting that memo apparently, he continues, "Are there going to be panties joining this dress on my floor tonight?" Okay, we've officially crossed over from gross to creepy. I squirm, trying to put some space between us, but he takes it as encouragement, trailing his hand down my dress and inches it up my thigh. When I put my hands on top of his to stop him, he grips my thigh hard enough that it might bruise.

"Come on, honey. The way you were grinding all over this dick tells me how much you want it."

"Um, no," I assert as I try to separate from him again. I manage to get a step away, but he turns me and grabs my forearms.

"Listen, thanks for the dance, but this," I say, pointing between us, "is not happening."

Moving closer into my space, his eyes get a predatory gleam. Searching for Kim and his friend, I realize they joined Haley on the side of the dancefloor, and we're isolated in the corner, backed up against the mirrors. "Don't be a cocktease. How about we get you another drink and see what you think then?" he suggests. As if another drink will make me go home with someone who smells like he drank the entire bar and insulted me.

I shake my head, but before I can get out a verbal response, he's gone. He was ripped away so violently that my body spun to face the mirror as I hear yelling behind me. The relief that hits me from his absence is short-lived when I gaze into the mirror and make eye contact with the person who pulled him away. A person I never thought I'd see again: the man who broke my heart four years ago, Robby Becker.

Instead of saying 'thank you' like a normal person, I turn around to make sure what I am seeing is, in fact, real and not my imagination. Once I confirm I am face-to-face with Robby, my fight-or-flight instinct kicks in. Usually, I freeze, but this time my body chooses flight and gets the hell out of dodge. One second, I am locked into Robby's ocean-blue eyes, and the next, I am standing with Haley and Kim. The guy's ginger friend is nowhere in sight.

"Are you okay?" They both yell at the same time. Shaking my head no, then yes, then no, the lump in my throat finally lessens.

"Can we go?" I ask shakily. They both agree. "Thank you! I'm going to run to the bathroom and wash that slime ball off me. Y'all call an Uber, and I'll meet you out front."

I'm introspective as I wash up in the bathroom. You'd think it's because of the altercation with that creep, but it isn't. It's due to a whole different interaction altogether. I'm blaming the fluttering of my heart – and dampness in my panties – on the drinks. It has nothing to do with the 6 '4" ghost from my past who just went all knight and shining armor on that shady perv. It absolutely has nothing to do with the way his muscles bunched as he flung around that jerkwad in defense of me. Nope. These tingles are a result of tequila. That's my story, and I'm sticking to it.

ACKNOWLEDGMENTS

Novellas are hard and this one of no exception. I am thankful for everyone who helped me through the process:

My Menaci for dealing with my late night spiraling
My wonderful beta reader, Jennifer, who helped me add more life to my characters
My editor for fitting in an emergency dev edit
My baddies for always responding to a "red" call
And last but not least, my loyal readers and book community who cheered me on during my first attempt outside my baseball world

ABOUT THE AUTHOR

Kat Summers is a millennial spicy, contemporary romance author living in Tennessee. Her books are filled with just enough angst to hurt your feelings, witty banter to make you laugh, and steamy, swoon-worthy men to make you blush. She creates stories with strong, sassy heroines who can hold their own but love being called a "good girl."

When she isn't writing, she can be found reading (duh) and spending time with her family and furbaby or gossiping over Mexican food. Fueled by Diet Dr Pepper and a dream, Kat is excited to bring the couples that live in her mind to the rest of the world. Follow her for sneak peeks of future projects.

Find her at @katsummerswrites on all the things.

ALSO BY KAT SUMMERS

Nashville Songbirds Series

Filled with sexy athletes and strong females leads, this sports romance series follows players of the Nashville Songbirds baseball team, the women they fall for, and a few friends along the way. Prepare for witty banter, heart and panty melting MMCs, and plenty of spice.

Currently, there are eight books planned in the Nashville Songbirds series, so if your favorite player doesn't have a story yet, follow me on social media (@katsummerswrites) for new book announcements!

Zealous Intentions

In order to land the biggest client of her career, workaholic Molly needs help from the flirty tattoo artist who has had his eye on her since they first met. Will this tatted cinnamon roll MMC get the girl? With a little fake dating and a whole lot of spice, he just might.